CITED TO DEATH

A Jamie Brodie Mystery

Chapter 1
Tuesday, May 29, 2012

"Hey, do you know a librarian named Daniel Christensen?"

"Yeah, why?"

"Because he's dead."

I set down the syrup with a thump and stared across the table at my brother. Obituaries with breakfast: one of the joys of rooming with a homicide detective. "It can't be the one I know. Dan's not even 40 yet."

Kevin folded the paper into quarters and handed it across the table to me. "Thirty-seven. Take a look."

CHRISTENSEN, Daniel W., 37, of Glendale, passed away suddenly on May 25, 2012. He was a graduate of CSU-Northridge and UCLA, and was a librarian at Cedars-Sinai Medical Center. He is survived by his parents, William and Brenda Christensen, his sister, Eliza Melendez, and his nieces, Sarah and Lindsey. Arrangements are pending.

Oh my God. I lay the paper down, stunned. "I knew him from library school. We had classes together during my first semester."

"Were you all friends?"

"Yeah, but I haven't seen him in years. This is unbelievable. I wonder if he'd been sick?"

"It says he died suddenly, right?"

"Right. Doesn't that mean heart attack, usually? He's kind of young for that."

"Not necessarily, if he's pushing 40." Kevin took the paper back and scanned the obituary again. "How well did you know him?"

"Pretty well. He was the first gay guy I met after I moved here. He was looking for a good time, and it had been a while for me, you know? I think I was a novelty to him, me the jock academic, but we both got tired of the novelty pretty fast."

"How'd he get to be a medical librarian?"

"Same way I got to be a history librarian. He already had a degree in something medical. As I remember, he was an RN."

"So you were more than friends."

"We slept together, if you consider that being more than friends. We didn't have much in common. He was into the leather scene and wanted to hang out with bikers and bondage types. I didn't find that appealing."

"But you fooled around with him anyway."

I glared at Kevin. "Stop the interrogation. It only lasted one semester. Then he broke up with me and we both moved on. I don't know what became of him after that."

Kevin resumed scanning the death notices. "I don't remember meeting him."

"Because you didn't. He didn't like cops. Just one of the many things we didn't have in common." We'd argued about it. "It wasn't a sustainable relationship."

"Sustainable relationship. I like that. Have to use that in a sentence today. 'The suspect blew her old man away because it wasn't a sustainable relationship.' Whaddya think?"

"I think that's not a very good excuse for murder."

Kevin snorted. "There almost never is." He waved his fork at my plate. "Finish up. Your pancakes are getting cold."

I poked at my pancakes with my fork. "I'm not that hungry."

"Eat anyway. You're only a week out of the hospital. You have to get your strength back."

Kevin's girlfriend, Abby, came out of their bedroom. She was dressed in jeans and a t-shirt, ready for work doing set construction at one of the studios. She overheard Kevin's last remark. "He's right, you know." She dug in her bag for her keys. "And breakfast is the most important meal, blah blah blah." She bent down to kiss Kevin and then patted me on the head. I swatted at her hand and she laughed. "See you tonight, guys."

Kevin saw her out the door, then sat back down and tapped me on the hand with his fork. "You sure you're ready to go back to work?"

"I have to go back. I told Dr. Loomis I'd be back today. If I don't show up, she'll come looking for me."

"Okay, then, but take it easy. Pace yourself this week. You don't want a relapse."

I stuck my tongue out at him. "Yes, Dad."

He just laughed.

I left the apartment and headed toward campus. After Kevin got divorced and I moved to LA, we'd chosen an apartment in Westwood based on convenience. I could walk to work, and Kevin and Abby both had reasonably short drives.

I enjoyed my daily trek across campus. On the way to work, it let me get into the library mindset and think about what I needed to do that day. On the way home, it let me clear my head and decompress. I had a car, an old VW bug, but I didn't have to use it very often.

Today, though, I wasn't thinking about what I was going to face when I got to work. I was thinking about Dan.

Dan had been a rebound relationship for me, several months after my breakup with Ethan, my boyfriend through college and grad school. Ethan had broken my heart, and Dan wasn't interested in that part of my anatomy. I'd liked him; he was smart and funny. We both enjoyed old monster movies and baseball. But he was secretive and had an unpredictable temper. We'd never gone on a date; we'd only hung out at his place, and always ended up in bed. He started experimenting with BDSM at the leather clubs, and wanted me to join in. I said no. He gave me an ultimatum, I said no again, and he broke up with me, right before Christmas.

Dan was working full time as a nurse, and moved through library school more slowly than I did. We never had another class together after that first semester. I heard through the grapevine that he started seeing another guy almost immediately after he broke up with me. Even though I'd known that Dan wasn't a good candidate for happily-ever-after with me, that stung. Probably because Ethan had left me for someone else too. I'd see Dan around the research library occasionally, until he graduated and took the job at Cedars three years ago. I hadn't seen him since.

And now I never would again.

Thoughts of Dan were dispelled as soon as I walked in the door of the library. I'd been out for two weeks after a severe asthma attack, complicated by bronchitis. I'd kept in touch via email, but everyone greeted me like I'd just returned from two months in the Himalayas. It took me nearly twenty minutes to pick up the day's mail and make it up the stairs to my office.

When I got there, I found a mess. For two weeks, someone had been dumping my mail in my office, stacking it up wherever they could find a bare spot. My desk was covered in books and papers. The bulk of it was probably junk, but some of it was books and articles that I'd requested through interlibrary loan for our history faculty. It was all stacked haphazardly, covering my desk completely in a blizzard of paper, and drifting like snow over the sides onto the floor. I had a chair for visitors in front of my desk, and I could barely see it under the piles of stuff. There was even a slumping stack on my own desk chair. I couldn't sit down until I cleared it off.

Damn. I had my work cut out for me. I turned on my computer and cleared the seat of my chair, dumping that stack on the floor beside me.

My computer was still booting up and I was gloomily surveying the mess when Liz Nguyen knocked on my door. Liz was one of my fellow reference librarians and my closest friend on staff. She was 29. Half Hawaiian, one quarter Vietnamese and one quarter

French, and 100% gorgeous – even I could appreciate that. She'd graduated a year behind me from library school, and was my partner on the reference desk for our 1-3 pm shift. "How are you feeling?"

"Much better. What's up?"

She came in and looked around at the mess. "Good Lord. This disaster happened in just two weeks?"

"Apparently. I was just starting to go through it."

Liz shook her head. "I bet a bunch of those catalogs are from Pacey Press. Harley Buhrman's been calling every day, wanting to know when you'd be back. He scheduled an appointment for next Monday."

Harley Buhrman was the LA-area sales rep for Pacey Press, a small publisher of reference books. The company was one of the slowest in adapting to the digital age; they had just released their first electronic database last year. They produced scholarly, beautiful, expensive sets of history encyclopedias that no one wanted to buy anymore. He'd been calling me every day before I went out sick. "Great. Who scheduled that?"

"Roberta. He came in and brought her a box of chocolates."

Roberta was the staff assistant to the senior administrative assistant to the director of the library. She had a sweet tooth and definitely could be bribed. She was also the most likely suspect in the case of my office mail dump. Roberta didn't like me. I sighed. "I guess it was inevitable."

"You weren't going to be able to put him off forever. At least it's not until next week."

"Thanks. It'll probably take me until then to sort through all this and find one of his catalogs."

Liz laughed and went back to her office. I added the appointment to my calendar for next Monday then checked my email; there was nothing important pending. Fortunately, I had a pretty clear day in front of me. The first thing I had to do was get through this mail and find the ILL requests. I'd been working in a groove for about an hour, separating books, articles, and junk into stacks, when someone darkened my door. “Hey, you! Back to the salt mines, eh?”

I looked up to see Diane DeLong leaning against the door frame. Diane had been in my library school cohort, and we’d remained friendly, although I wouldn’t call her a close friend. In school, she’d been the class gossip. Telephone, telegraph, tell Diane. Somehow she’d found out that I was in the hospital, and had descended on my room daily to “cheer me up.” She was a high school librarian in Pasadena, and was just starting her summer vacation. Diane was a lifelong Goth, with punk tendencies. She was dressed in black from head to toe, except for her lime green Mohawk.

“Hey, yourself. What are you doing here? And how did they let you in?”

Diane smirked. “I don’t think your boss saw me. As to what I’m doing here...” She picked up a stack of paper and sat down. “I’ve got some bad news, and I wanted to tell you in person. You might want to sit down too.”

I sat. “If it’s about Dan Christensen, I know. I saw his obituary in the paper this morning.”

“Ah. You guys were involved, weren’t you?”

“We were - um - kind of – do you know what happened to him?”

“My sister-in-law is a nurse at Cedars, and she said they’re not sure, but they think it was a seizure. He had seizures, didn’t he?”

I remembered a row of prescription bottles in Dan’s medicine cabinet. “Yeah. He did. But he was at work? How did no one see it?”

“Apparently he’d stayed at work late on Friday evening. The cleaning crew found him yesterday morning when they opened his office.”

“I can’t believe this. He’d been there since Friday night?”

“They think so. The library isn’t open on the weekends. The police came, but they said it wasn’t a suspicious death.”

“Had you kept in touch with him?”

"To some extent. But I didn't see him very often." Diane looked sympathetic. "Were you guys very close?"

"Not really. We just fooled around some. And it was only for four months. After graduation I never saw him again."

Diane made a disapproving face. "Hmph. You're going to the funeral, aren't you?"

"I hadn't planned to."

"I think we should. I don't think Dan had many friends. It would be nice for his family if a few people who knew him and didn't hate him showed up."

"When is the service? And where?"

"It's a graveside service. Forest Lawn in Glendale. Thursday afternoon, 2:30."

"I don't know if I can take any more leave. I've been gone for two weeks."

"So check with your boss. It's not all day, it's just a couple of hours. Do you have anything scheduled that afternoon?"

I pulled up my calendar. "No."

"Go ask her. I'll wait." Diane leaned back, looking smug.

I sighed. Dr. Loomis was a force to be reckoned with, but so was Diane. I decided the request would go down better in person, and went downstairs to Dr. Loomis's office.

Madeline Loomis was my supervisor, the head of reference and instruction for the research library. She was a tiny woman, but formidable. She looked like an old school librarian, with her bun of gray hair and her glasses on a cord around her neck, but she was the first to encourage us to adapt technology into our work. She carried her iPad around with her like a totem and used it for everything. She was an excellent boss. Our love for her was only slightly tinged by fear.

Dr. Loomis was in her office, alone, with the door open. This was my lucky day. "Good morning, Dr. Loomis."

She looked up and smiled. "Jamie! Welcome back. Come in, sit down. How are you feeling?"

"Not bad. Almost back to normal."

She narrowed her eyes at me. "But not entirely back to normal."

"Well, no. I still don't have a lot of energy. But that will resolve itself now that I'm back to work."

She leaned back in her chair and crossed her arms. "Jamie. You still have more sick leave accumulated than anyone in this building. I want you to promise me that if you don't feel up to working, you won't come in. I'm already impressed with your work ethic. You don't have to keep impressing me with it. Understood?"

"Yes, ma'am."

She nodded sharply. "All right. Now that we have that clear, what can I do for you?"

"One of my library school classmates passed away over the weekend. His memorial service is Thursday afternoon in Glendale. I don't have anything else scheduled and I'd like to use a couple of hours of personal time. If that's okay."

Dr. Loomis looked surprised. "My goodness. Was this anyone I would know?"

"I don't know. His name was Dan Christensen. He was the medical librarian at Cedars-Sinai."

"Hmm. No, I don't believe that name is familiar. I'm so sorry. Had he been ill?"

"No, ma'am. They think it was a seizure. He had a seizure disorder."

"Goodness." Dr. Loomis's mouth compressed in a thin line for a moment. She looked as if she was remembering something unpleasant. "Of course you may take the time. Just get me your leave form by the end of the day."

"Yes ma'am, I will. Thank you."

"You're welcome. And welcome back. Please take care of yourself. If you find you can't finish out the day and need to leave early, don't hesitate to do that."

I smiled. "I don't think that will be a problem. But thank you."

I went back upstairs. Diane was behind my desk, doing – what? Sorting mail? She straightened up as I came in. "What did she say?"

"She said yes. What are you doing?"

"Helping. I got bored. So, good! We can go to the funeral. Do you want me to come pick you up?"

"If you don't mind. Then I don't have to move the Bug."

"I don't mind. I'll call you when I get close to campus and meet you outside somewhere."

"Sounds good." I saw Diane off and turned back to my sorting.

Just before 1:00, I got a mochaccino at Café 451, the coffee shop on the first floor, then went to the desk for my reference shift. I sat down at the desk and smiled in anticipation. I had missed this.

I rubbed my hands together and grinned at Liz. "Let the questions and answers begin!"

She laughed. "You, sir, are a nut."

We were fairly busy. There were two weeks left in the quarter before finals, and the worst of the procrastinators were starting to do their research for their final papers and projects. And, right on the dot of 1:30, Clinton appeared.

Every library has its group of regular patrons that can be lumped together under the heading "eccentric." Academic libraries have two main types of eccentrics: needy students who latch on to an individual librarian, and conspiracy theorists from the community that come in to look for research to support their theories. We had a few others: the dominatrix who came in each evening wearing her work clothes to read the Wall Street Journal, the student who was a Civil War re-enactor and came in every Friday in full Confederate uniform, the graduate student who claimed to be in the Witness Protection program.

And we had Clinton.

We didn't know anything about Clinton. We didn't even know if Clinton was his first or last name. Every afternoon at 1:30, Clinton would approach the reference desk and stand, waiting patiently, until one of us was free. Liz or I would say, "Hi, Clinton," and he'd say, very gravely, "The word of the day is _________" and give us a word. Then he'd bow from the waist and walk away.

He'd been doing this for as long as Liz and I had been partners on the reference desk.

When I saw him, I said, "Hi, Clinton."

He looked at me somberly. "The word for the day is *nomothetic*." Then he bowed and walked away.

Liz looked it up. "It means 'Giving or establishing laws; legislative.'"

"Okay." I recorded it in the spiral notebook that we used as a log for Clinton's words.

At 3:00, I went back to my office and resumed sorting mail. By the time 5:00 rolled around, I was exhausted. I was determined to get through today's mail, though; if I could keep up with the new stuff, I'd be able to chip away at the old stuff without anything else piling up.

I was just moving today's stack of mail to my desk when there was a knock on my door frame. I looked up into the deep brown eyes of Pete Ferguson.

When I first moved to LA, Pete was my brother Kevin's partner on the police force. After Dan broke up with me, I'd had a string of similarly short-term relationships, and Pete was one of them. He'd left the force by then, and was pursuing a Ph.D. in psychology at UCLA. We'd gotten along great. But Pete had a bad breakup in his past too, and we'd both been afraid of getting hurt again. Then Pete's ex had come back and wanted a second chance, and Pete had reluctantly given it to him. By the time Luke and Pete had broken up for good, I'd moved on. Pete's friendship with Kevin had kept us in contact, and we'd re-established a cautious friendship of our own.

Now here he was, standing in my doorway. I tried to smile; it must have looked more like a grimace. "Hey, what are you doing here?"

Pete smiled back. He had a dazzling smile. "I wanted to see if I could buy you dinner on your way home. Figured you'd be done for the day by now."

I was suddenly suspicious. "Did Kevin send you here?"

"No, I've been here all afternoon doing research. But it did occur to me that you might need some encouragement to leave work on time, and maybe I could entice you away."

"Doing research? I thought the point of taking a teaching job at a community college was so you didn't have to do research."

Pete laughed. He had a nice laugh too. "I don't have to, but it does help with tenure. And the professor who was my dissertation adviser here has asked me to write a chapter for a textbook that she's editing. Hence the need for research."

"A textbook on what?"

"Abnormal psychology. My chapter's on criminal psychology. And right now I'm criminally hungry. So whaddya say? How does Thai sound?"

"It sounds great. I just want to go through this last stack of mail before I leave. Have a seat."

Pete moved a stack off the chair and sat. "This place is a mess."

"No kidding. They've just been throwing my mail in here as it came."

"Nice. I hope there wasn't anything important in it."

"Probably not." I was tossing catalogs into my chair and important-looking mail in the direction of my inbox on my desk. None of it looked interesting, until I came to an envelope with a name I recognized. It stopped me in my tracks.

Holy shit. I must have had an odd look on my face. Pete noticed. "What's wrong?"

"This morning I found out that this guy I used to know died. And now here's a letter from him. It's postmarked the day before he died."

"Who is it?"

"Dan Christensen. We started library school together. He's a medical librarian at Cedars now. *Was* a medical librarian. He died on Friday."

"Christensen. Why does that name sound familiar?"

"I was kind of - um - involved with him for a while. You might have heard me mention him." I looked narrowly at Pete. "That was almost six years ago. If you remember that, you've got an awfully good memory."

"Hey, I've always paid attention to your love life." He nodded at the letter. "What does he want?"

I looked at the letter again. It was postmarked Malibu. *Malibu?* Dan lived in Glendale and worked in LA. Why would he mail something from Malibu? I opened it and pulled out a sheet of paper.

It was a page torn off a yellow legal pad, not hospital stationery. I read out loud. "Jamie - if anything happens to me, check this out." I stopped at what was below that sentence. "What the..."

"What is it?"

I handed the letter to Pete. "'If anything happens to me…' What's he talking about?"

Pete examined the note. "What's this at the bottom? It looks like journal citations."

It was. Below Dan's note, he had written two citations.

The first seemed to be in a foreign language:

Hughes, D., & Llewellyn, M. (2003). Nid yw symbylu'r celloedd bonyn embryonig dynol diwylliedig â hormonau ffoligl ysgogol yn arwain at ffurfio ofwm tebyg i gelloedd. *Meddygol Cymru Journal, 17*(9), 23-28.

The second was in English, but was nearly as incomprehensible as the first:

> **Oliver, T., Wray, A., & Goldstein, B. (2007). Stimulation of cultured human embryonic stem cells with follicle stimulating hormone leads to formation of ovum-like cells. *Journal of Stem Cell Biology, 2*(4), 15-22.**

"This looks like medical stuff. How am I supposed to read this?"

"What language is that?"

"The names could be Welsh. And Cymru means Wales. I think it's Welsh language."

"Can you read it?"

"No."

"You could run it through Google Translate to get an idea of what it says. Why would he send this to you? You're not a medical librarian."

"I don't know. I might be the only librarian he knows in the UC system. Or maybe he thought… Oh hell, I don't *know*."

"And those are just citations. Why wouldn't he have sent you the articles themselves?"

"I have no idea. Maybe he couldn't find the full text." I grimaced. "This is creepy. Dan's *dead*. Do you think someone might have done something to him?"

"Like what? Was there anything to indicate foul play?"

"No. The obituary just said he died suddenly. And what could be dangerous about a couple of medical articles?" I frowned at the paper in my hand.

"You could ask Kevin about it. He can get the police report and the autopsy results. See if there was anything off about it."

I frowned again. "I guess. But that'll take a while, won't it?"

"Yeah, it won't be a priority." Pete picked up my computer bag from the floor. "Come on, I'm hungry. You can fill me in on this guy and those listings while we eat."

We walked to a Thai place near campus. Once in our booth we ordered beer and pad thai; our beers arrived almost immediately. Pete took a drink and leaned back. "Tell me about this Dan guy. I don't remember ever meeting him."

"You didn't. He never came home with me. We didn't really date. It was mostly physical, and it only lasted for four months."

Pete studied me. "That doesn't sound like your kind of thing."

"It wasn't. But he was the first gay guy I met after I moved back here. And I hadn't been with anyone for almost a year since Ethan left, and no strings attached sounded good to me at the time."

"You had met me."

"Yeah, but there was the small matter of Luke."

I couldn't interpret the look on his face. "Back to Dan. Tell me more about him."

"What, you want to do a psychological profile?"

"Why not?"

I took another drink. "Dan Christensen. Tall, skinny, Teutonic looking. He joined the army right out of high school, was a medic and got assigned to Germany. He was in five years then was in a bad car crash over there, had a head injury, developed a seizure disorder and had to take a medical discharge. He came back here, went to nursing school on the GI bill, worked at County in the ER for four years, and then decided to get a library degree. He kept working in the ER to put himself through school, so it took him longer and he graduated a year after me. He got the librarian job at Cedars as soon as he graduated. I'd see him around campus until then, but haven't seen him at all for three years."

"So it's odd that he sent you this letter."

"Yes."

"What was he like?"

I sighed. "He was hard to read. He could be funny and joke around, then something would set him off and he'd fly off the handle. He had a lot of tattoos and piercings and was adding to them all the time. We didn't see each other on the weekends because if he wasn't working he was at the leather bars in West Hollywood. I always thought that might be a phase, like he was still figuring out what it meant to him to be gay. He was very intelligent, but he did just enough in school to get by. He said library school was only a hoop to jump through to get the piece of paper that said you were a librarian, and there wasn't any point in straining himself to do well, he'd get the same piece of paper that the rest of us had."

"So he could be a jerk."

"Yeah. He didn't have a lot of friends at school."

"And you broke it off after your first semester."

"He broke it off. He wanted to try out the BDSM clubs, and I wouldn't go with him, so he chose that over me. But in March I met Nick, and I got over it."

"Which one was Nick?"

"Film student. Wore his hair in a braid."

"Oh, yeah. So how bad was Dan's seizure disorder?"

"I don't really know. He took meds for it. I don't think he was supposed to drive, but he did. I never knew of him having any seizures when we were in school, at least."

"Hmm. His personality fits that of someone who's had a head injury. The outbursts, the socially inappropriate behavior, the risk taking. And maybe, based on that note, paranoia."

"Could be." I reminisced for a moment. "I remember him saying that he didn't miss the army because he had gotten tired of taking orders from asshole officers, and he wouldn't miss the ER because he was tired of taking orders from asshole doctors. So he wasn't good at subordination, even though he was a sub at the BDSM clubs. It didn't match."

"Which was probably one of the sources of his anger. Confusion. Cognitive dissonance. Self-hatred. Possibly consistent with the piercings."

"On top of that, his family had completely disowned him when he came back from Germany and told them he was gay. His parents were strict Baptists or something and didn't want anything else to do with him. He always said that was no big deal, but he still lived in Glendale where he had grown up."

"Lots of contradictions there."

"He was a complicated guy."

"So - why do you think he sent you this letter? Why would it matter that you're a UC librarian?"

"Because I have access to resources that other librarians don't? That's the only reason I can think of."

Our food came, and we dug in and talked about other things. Pete had parked on the street near our apartment building, and we said goodbye at his car.

Neither Kevin nor Abby were home yet. No surprise there. I changed clothes and got a beer out of the fridge, booted up my laptop, and opened Google Translate. I spread Dan's letter in front of me and typed the first citation, minus the names and date, into the "From: Detect Language" box. Immediately the box changed to "From: Welsh-detected," and the translation read:

Does not stimulate human embryonic stem cells cultured with follicle stimulating hormone leads to the formation of ovum-like cells. Medical Journal

I compared it to the second citation from the letter. The words were similar, but the sentence was so scrambled it was impossible to make any sense from it. I copied and pasted the two article titles and compared them side by side.

Does not stimulate human embryonic stem cells cultured with follicle stimulating hormone leads to the formation of ovum-like cells.

Stimulation of cultured human embryonic stem cells with follicle stimulating hormone leads to formation of ovum-like cells.

I leaned back and regarded the citations for a minute. The first one was like a jigsaw puzzle, or one of those jumble word games they put in the newspaper. I just needed to unscramble it. I started lining up phrases that matched, and finally had an order that made a little sense:

Stimulate cultured human embryonic stem cells with follicle stimulating hormone does not leads to the formation of ovum-like cells.

A couple of grammatical fixes later, I had:

Stimulation of cultured human embryonic stem cells with follicle stimulating hormone does not lead to formation of ovum-like cells.

I looked at the title from the second article again. The titles were identical, except for one word. *Not.* The first researchers found that their procedure didn't work, and the second group found that it did. That didn't sound unusual. Medical research was changing all the time. One week coffee was bad for you, the next week it was good. Why would this be any different?

I failed to see the mystery in this. What was Dan thinking?

At any rate, there wasn't anything else I could do about it tonight. And I was really tired. I saved the citations to Dropbox and got ready for bed.

Once in bed, though, I couldn't go to sleep. My brain wouldn't shut down. Thoughts of Pete, Dan, and the letter kept swirling through.

For the first time since we'd dated, Pete and I were both single at the same time. Did he want to get back together? Did *I?* I didn't think so. My latest boyfriend, Scott, had broken up with me while I was in the hospital two weeks ago. I might become a monk. *They have libraries in monasteries, don't they?* I purposely hadn't gotten firmly attached to any guy since Ethan so that when they left me, as I knew they would, it wouldn't hurt. But the routine was getting old. I didn't think I could maintain the detachment with Pete, and when he left me it would hurt a lot. So I couldn't go there.

I rolled from my side to my back, stared at the ceiling and thought about Dan. Was he simply paranoid, and his death a weird coincidence? Or did he have reason to be paranoid? And why would he send the letter to *me?* Why make a dying request of someone you hadn't contacted for years? Why not ask another medical librarian? I knew every history librarian in California; Dan had to know at least a few other medical librarians. Surely one of them would be better equipped to solve this puzzle than I was.

Maybe he *had* sent the letter to other people as well. But how would I know?

History has two functions: serving as a record of what happened and analyzing why it happened. I didn't know *why* Dan sent me the letter, but I did have *what* he sent me. Two titles, separated by one word. On the surface, there was nothing suspicious about that. So if the answer to *why* wasn't in the titles, maybe it was in the text of the articles.

That gave me a plan of action. Tomorrow, I'd look for the full text of the articles. If I was right in speculating that Dan had sent the letter to me because I was a UC librarian, then I'd put the power of the UC library system to work.

With that settled, I drifted off to sleep.

Chapter 2
Wednesday, May 30

I was feeling pretty good the next morning, and went for a swim before work. I had three goals for the day. First, I had to finish going through the mail and get the interlibrary loan materials delivered. It wasn't necessary to do that in person, but it was a good way for me to keep in touch with the history faculty, to remind them that they had their own subject librarian at their disposal. That took most of the morning, and it wasn't until almost 11:00 that I was able to focus on my second goal: finding the full text of the citations Dan had given me.

I opened up our citation linker and typed in the second title first. It popped up, but only the abstract was available to me. I read it; I was unsure of most of the jargon, but it looked like a typical medical research article. For the full text, I needed a separate log in for the biomedical library, which I didn't have.

I went back to the citation linker and typed in the first title, first in English and then in Welsh. No hits on either. So I was going to have to visit the biomed library.

I let Liz know where I was going, and headed south. UCLA's hospital and medical school complex is spread across the south end of campus, and the Research Library is at the north end. It was a pleasant day for a walk. I went into the biomedical library and was glad to see Karen Lewis at the reference desk. Karen and I had served on a couple of committees together, and she'd always been friendly. She spotted me and waved.

"Jamie Brodie! We are graced with the presence of the humanities!"

I laughed. "Social sciences, to be exact. Got a minute?"

"Sure. What's up?"

I laid my printout of the two citations, including the translation of the Welsh title, in front of her. "I've got a mystery to clear up, and I need the full text of these. Google Translate gave me the English version of this title, or at least a reasonable facsimile. The language is Welsh."

"Huh." Karen looked at the two articles. "This is stem cell research. Looks like your Welsh guys were unsuccessful with this procedure, and the next guys were successful. There are four years between these two; I'd bet that the second one finally figured out how to do the procedure."

"That's kind of what I thought, but I wanted to make sure. A librarian friend of mine asked me to look these up, then he was found dead on Monday."

"*What*? Oh my God! Do you think there's some connection?"

"No. He had a seizure disorder, and apparently was alone at work on Friday evening and had a seizure and died. The library was closed on the weekend, so no one found him until Monday."

Karen frowned. "He was a librarian? Where?"

"Cedars. Dan Christensen. Did you know him?"

"The name is familiar. Was he active in any of the associations?"

"I don't know. We went through library school together, but I hadn't seen him since then."

"Why'd he ask you to do this?"

"I have no idea. I thought it might have been because I was the only UC librarian he knew."

Karen read the titles again. "This is pretty big stuff. It looks like what both groups were trying to do is create human egg cells out of stem cells. This would be hugely significant if it was possible."

"So this second group has figured out how to do it. Good for them."

"Yeah. Okay..." Karen turned to her computer and started clicking on things. "I'll do the easy one first. Here it is, right in Biological Record."

"I could see the abstract, but I couldn't log in for the full text."

"No problem." Karen printed the article and handed it to me. "Now… Boy, Welsh is an odd language. Can you find someone to translate the article for you?"

"I think so. If Google Translate can't handle it, I've got friends at Oxford that can either do it or know someone who can."

"Ooooh, friends at Oxford." Karen smirked. "Okay, we don't have it. I'll have to put in an ILL request."

"That's fine. There's obviously no rush."

Karen studied her screen. "It's only held by three libraries in the world. Lucky for you, one of them is Oxford."

"Excellent. If you have trouble getting them to send it, let me know and I'll rattle some cages."

"Ha ha." Karen did some more typing and clicking, then sat back. "Your ILL request is on its way. You know this will take a while."

"I know. Will they send it electronically?"

"Probably. Either way, it will come right to you."

"Okey dokey." I stood up. "Ms. Lewis, you rock. A thousand thank yous."

Karen grinned. "You owe me one. And don't be a stranger! We need a little more humanity around this place."

After I left the biomedical library, I had a meeting to attend. I was on a curriculum development committee for the library school, which was quartered in the building next to the research library. I sat through the meeting, but my mind wasn't fully on it. I was anxious to take a look at the article burning a hole in my bag.

When I got back to my office, my monitor screen was blank. That was weird; it was set up to run a screen saver, not go into power save mode like that. I jiggled the mouse, expecting my desktop layout to reappear. It didn't. I looked at the power indicator; the light on the start button was off. I turned the computer back on and waited. Instead of the usual booting up sequence, I saw the thing feared by computer users everywhere - the dreaded blue screen of death. My hard drive had crashed. *Shit.*

I called IT and left my information on their automated system. The recorded voice assured me that someone would be in touch to address my problem in a timely manner. I hung up and considered my options. I only had about 15 minutes until I was due on the reference desk, so it didn't make much sense to commandeer someone else's computer, or get my laptop fired up in that amount of time. I stashed my laptop in my filing cabinet and locked it, hit the coffee shop for a little pick me up, and headed for reference.

At 1:30, Clinton walked up to the desk.

I said, "Hi, Clinton."

"The word for the day is *spruik*." He bowed and walked away.

Liz looked it up. "To make or give a speech, especially extensively."

I laughed. "Well, we don't have to worry about that from Clinton."

I checked my email one more time before I left the reference computer at 3:00 and saw an email from Karen Lewis.

Hi Jamie,

Just wanted to let you know I got an acknowledgement of your request. The article should arrive next week. Much more quickly than I expected.

FYI, I just had a visit from one of the authors of the article I printed for you. The first author, as I remember – a Dr. Oliver. He was interested to know who wanted his article. Apparently he has an alert set up to ping him every time the article is downloaded. Can you imagine? I think he believed that one of our docs was going to use his procedure, the way he acted at first, but when he found out it was someone else he relaxed and became quite charming. I gave him your name, but he truly didn't seem interested once I told him it wasn't a medical person.

Cheers,

Karen

Shit. I wished she hadn't mentioned my name. But it didn't occur to me to tell her not to, because it didn't occur to me that anyone connected to the articles would find out. So the guy received an alert every time someone accessed his article? I didn't even know that was possible. Either he was really paranoid about having his work copied, or he had a huge ego and the alert was just a way to stroke it.

When I got back to my office, IT hadn't arrived yet, and my desktop PC was still dead. The top of my desk was clear after yesterday's cleaning binge, so I pushed the PC to the far side and opened my laptop. My third goal for the day was to finish work on a budget presentation that I was scheduled to give on Friday. I'd worked on it at home while I was recovering, so it was nearly complete. It just needed a few finishing touches. I kept all my works-in-progress in Dropbox so that I could access them from anywhere. The death of my PC was annoying but not a disaster because there was very little saved on its hard drive. All of my important files were in various clouds.

I finished up the PowerPoint slides I wanted to use and was in the process of transferring them to Prezi when there was a knock on the door. I looked up and saw a stranger. Silver hair, patrician features, expensive tailored suit, *very* expensive shoes. He smiled and held out his hand. "Dr. Brodie? I'm Tristan Oliver, of Fertility Research. Your medical librarian gave me your name."

Holy shit. I glanced at the clock over Oliver's shoulder on the opposite wall. I'd only been in Karen's office five hours earlier. This guy worked fast. I tried to keep my facial expression neutral.

Oliver's handshake was firm, dry, and brisk. "I understand from Ms. Lewis that you have an interest in an article that I coauthored."

Right to the point. "Yes, sir. Is there a problem?"

Oliver smiled. He had a politician's smile – not quite natural. "Not at all. Initially I was concerned that another medical group intended to co-opt our research. We have patents in place to prevent that, of course. Ms. Lewis assured me that you had no such intent. But I remained curious. What interest could a – I believe she said your subject was history, correct? What interest could a history librarian have in our research?"

Don't mention Dan. I tried to think fast. "Another librarian mentioned it to me in passing at a conference several months ago." The state library association met back in November; that would work as a ruse. "I thought it sounded interesting and wrote down the information, but it got lost in the shuffle and I just found my note yesterday. Karen was kind enough to print out the article for me."

Oliver seemed satisfied. He smiled again, a bit more warmly this time. "Do you have a particular interest in fertility medicine? For personal reasons, perhaps?"

Heh. Good one. "No, sir. I just wanted to expand my horizons. It keeps my brain sharp to read research from outside my field."

Oliver chuckled. He was charming when he wasn't in interrogation mode. "Very good, young man. Expand away. If you have any questions, feel free to contact me. My email address is listed on the paper."

"Yes, sir. I appreciate that."

"It's been a long time since anyone addressed me as sir. You must have been raised in a military household."

"Yes, sir. Marines."

"Excellent." Oliver looked nostalgic. "I was a Navy man myself. Better food and no crawling through the mud. Was your father a Korean War vet, by any chance?"

"No, sir. Vietnam."

"Ah." Oliver looked less nostalgic. "I was out of the service by then. Well, Dr. Brodie, I won't take any more of your time. Thank you for your interest in my work, and please don't hesitate to contact me."

"I won't. Thank you, sir."

Oliver strode away.

I watched him go and let out a long breath; I'd been half holding it without realizing. Why would Oliver come in person for a five-minute conversation? Did he just want to make doubly sure that no one was going to steal his research? Or was there more to it?

It was 5:00. I taught a class on Wednesdays that started at 5:30, so I needed to get going. I was packing up when IT Andy appeared at the door. Andy Mitchell was the guy who usually came to work on our computers. We called him IT Andy to distinguish him from another Andy that worked at the circulation desk. He looked surprised to see me. "Hey, Dr. B. I didn't think you'd still be here."

"I was just leaving. I'm glad to see you."

Andy grinned. "I bet. What happened?"

"I was out of the office for a couple of hours, and when I came back, the computer had shut itself down. I turned it back on and got a blue screen."

"Huh. Let me take a look." He sat down at my desk and started clicking "Weird. It looks like your hard drive just gave up the ghost, but I'm not sure why. How old was it?"

I tried to remember. "I don't know. It's been a couple of years, I guess, since it was replaced? Doesn't it tell you in there somewhere?"

"Yeah, as soon as I can get it restored, I'll be able to tell. Probably the easiest thing will be to bring you a new hard drive, but I might be able to get this one back in working order. It will save most of your files if I can."

"Okay. Whatever it takes. You think you can get it done by morning?"

"Oh yeah. It'll be up and running when you get in tomorrow."

"Fantastic. Thanks, Andy."

He waved, already deep into IT guy mode. I left.

The class I was teaching this quarter, Historical Research Methods, was held in the education and information science building, right next door to the research library. This was our next-to-last class for the term. It was a 3 ½ hour class. I usually began with 30 to 45 minutes of lecture, then the students would have an in-class research activity to complete based on the lecture. Then we'd spend the last 45 minutes or so talking about what they'd found. Tonight's topic was California history, and the resources available for researching it. The students were on task, and we finished class about 20 minutes early. I answered a few questions about the final project that was due in two weeks, then headed home.

Even though it was dark, there were a lot of people around – night classes all let out at the same time. I'd never felt unsafe walking on campus after dark. Being 6'2" and 185 pounds had its advantages: not the most attractive target for a mugger. But tonight, I had a weird feeling that someone was following me. I looked back a couple of times and even stopped once to re-tie my shoes so that I could sneak a look behind me, but I didn't see anyone suspicious. I decided that I was letting the events of the day color my imagination. Why would anyone be following me?

When I got home, I found a note from Kevin. "At the movies." They'd be home before long. I changed into sweats and sat down on the sofa with Oliver's article and a medical dictionary I'd checked out of the library earlier today. An hour later, my eyes were crossing with exhaustion, and I'd managed to read through about a page and a half. This area of research might be a big deal, but it was dry reading for a non-medical person. I was starting to catch on to the terminology a bit, but I was too tired to continue.

Kevin and Abby came in as I was getting my computer bag ready for the following day. I said hello and chatted for a few minutes, then collapsed into bed. I'd tell Kevin about my visit from Dr. Oliver in the morning.

Chapter 3
Thursday, May 31

But I didn't get a chance to tell Kevin anything. When I got up at 5:30, he was already dressed and heading out the door, on the way to a crime scene.

The day dawned hot, hazy and humid, with an air quality alert. That was especially bad news on this day. People with asthma were supposed to stay indoors on days like this. Instead, I'd be heading towards the Valley, and the worst of the smog, to stand outside for at least 30 minutes. I usually went for a run on Thursdays, but because of the alert, I went to the pool instead.

I'd had asthma as a kid, but it got significantly worse when I moved to LA. The air in LA was a lot better than it used to be, but still not as good as in Oceanside, north of San Diego, where I'd grown up. Or Berkeley, where I'd gone to college. Or Oxford, England, where I'd gotten my doctorate. I had to use a preventive inhaler every day and carry a rescue inhaler with me wherever I went. I was sensitive to just about everything. Dust, smog, pollen, and cats were all no-nos. But the worst was perfume and cologne. Some brands just made me cough, but some made me start wheezing even before I could get my inhaler out of my pocket. Everyone knew not to wear scent around me. I even had a sign posted on my office door banning those wearing perfume, cologne, and other scents from entering.

As I left the house, I patted my pocket to make sure my inhaler was there.

When I got to the office, I had a voice mail waiting for me from Dr. Loomis. "Jamie – please come see me." *Oh shit.* What did I do?

I hustled downstairs and knocked at her door, and she beckoned me in. "Please come in and look at this."

Dr. Loomis's email was open, and it was full of messages from me. Most of them seemed to be offering Dr. Loomis the opportunity to invest in metals. I was appalled. "Holy sh- um – crap! How many of those are there?"

"At least 100. Charles and Lesley in Technical Services inform me that the same phenomenon has occurred in their email. I expect there will be others. Can I assume that you know nothing about this?"

"No, ma'am. I mean, yes, ma'am, you can assume that. I have no idea what's going on. My computer crashed yesterday, but I thought IT fixed it."

"Have you turned on your computer yet this morning?"

"No, I came straight here."

"Perhaps you should go check your own email. I have called IT to come look at mine; I'll send them to you when they finish here."

"Thank you. I'm really sorry about this." I headed back downstairs. What *was* going on? First my computer crashed yesterday, and now this. It flashed through my mind to wonder if it had anything to do with Dan's articles and the visit from Dr. Oliver. But I dismissed that immediately. That was eccentric-patron conspiracy theory land, and I wasn't going there. It had to be coincidence. No one from outside UCLA should be able to hack into the system deeply enough to affect only my computer, and no one from inside UCLA was involved in the Dan issue.

As I walked into the office, my phone was ringing. It was Karen Lewis. "Hey, Karen."

"Hey. Do you have a problem with your email?"

"Oh no, you've gotten carpet bombed too?"

"Oh yeah. Big time. Do you really think I should invest in a nickel mine?"

I snorted. "It looks like everyone in my internal address book has been getting spammed by me all night. Dr. Loomis called me in first thing about it. IT's on the way."

"Okay. Just wanted to see what was going on."

We said goodbye. I logged on to my computer and opened email, then files. Everything looked okay. My own email seemed to be unaffected, and there was nothing in my "sent" folder. However, I had messages from people all over the university telling me they were being spammed from my account. I wrote a group email to all of my contacts, explaining and apologizing. I didn't know what else to do.

In the meantime, I had to get some work done. I finalized my budget presentation and started working on collection development requests. I had switched my reference shift to the morning to accommodate the funeral, and the desk was busy. I ate the lunch I'd packed at my desk, still working.

I was supposed to meet Diane outside at 1:30. But, at 1:15, she appeared at my door. Her hair today was dyed a more funeral-appropriate maroon color. "Hey, ready to go?"

"I thought I was going to meet you outside. You didn't have to park and come in."

"It's okay. I found a parking spot without too much trouble." Diane looked around the office. "It looks a lot better in here than it did Tuesday."

"No kidding." I took my inhaler from my computer bag and locked the rest of the bag, including my laptop, in my filing cabinet. "I've got to visit the men's room. Then I'll be ready to go."

When I got back to my office, Diane was sitting at my desk, doing something on my computer. *What the hell?* "What the hell are you doing?"

Diane looked hurt. "I'm just checking my email. I didn't think it would be a problem."

"I didn't mean to snap at you, but it took me by surprise. My computer's been acting weird the past couple of days. It might have a virus."

"Oh – well, I use protection. I'm sure I won't catch it."

"Ha ha." I logged out of the PC and we left. It occurred to me that I'd caught Diane behind my desk twice now. Could *she* be involved in my computer issues? She was the only person I could think of that had used it besides me. But why would she do that?

I was still pondering that as Diane pulled out of the parking garage. But I didn't think long; Diane was her usual chatty self. She filled me in on all of our classmates, giving me far more detail than I wanted to know about any of them. "How do you know all this?"

"Facebook, duh. Speaking of, when are you going to get on there?"

"I'm not. I value my privacy."

"Oh, come on. How are you going to know what's going on with your friends and family?"

"Well, see, I have this great new device. It's called a cell phone. You can actually talk to people live, and not have to wait for them to update their status online. It's fun."

Diane glowered. "You're such a smart ass."

"It's a gift."

"Seriously. Don't you have nieces or nephews or something? How do you keep up with them?"

"I talk to them. On the phone. No one in my family is on Facebook or any other social media. We discussed it, and none of us are comfortable with it. Especially because my brother frequently causes people to go to jail for a long, long time, and some of them get disgruntled and might try to track us down. Besides, it's not like my nephews are in Timbuktu. They're in San Diego."

"That is just weird. It's practically un-American."

I expressed my opinion through sign language. She snorted. "You know, you and Dan had that in common. He wasn't on Facebook either."

"No surprise there."

"I guess not. Oh, look! Is that Lindsay Lohan?"

"Oh, for God's sake…"

When we got to Forest Lawn, Diane parked in the main lot by the mortuary. "There's a viewing inside first, and then they're going to hold the graveside service."

"A viewing? I didn't know anyone did those anymore."

"We can skip the viewing if it skeezes you out."

"No, it's okay. The more time I spend indoors the better."

We walked inside and I was hit in the face by the odor of dozens of bouquets of flowers. I groaned inwardly. The air quality was almost as bad in here as it was outside, as far as my lungs were concerned. We were directed into a small room, with a couple of dozen people standing around. One guy seemed to be the funeral director, and another a clergyman. A youngish man in a tailored suit was standing by himself, seemingly as far away from the casket as he could get. *Someone from the hospital?* I wondered. He didn't look like Dan's type. There were a couple of tattooed guys who did. An older couple, a woman around 40, and a couple of young teenage girls were sitting in folding chairs, perpendicular to the open casket.

"That must be the family." Diane elbowed me. "Let's go give our condolences."

We introduced ourselves. Dan's parents were both wispy and gray, holding themselves stiffly. His sister was overweight and harried-looking; the nieces looked bored. Dan's mother held onto my hand when I offered it. "Thank you both so much for coming. It's nice to know that Danny had friends who cared about him."

Diane stepped in smoothly. "Dan loved library work. It was a pleasure to have known him. We're so sorry about what happened."

We moved away from the family and approached the casket. I looked at Dan. He looked peaceful, much more so than he had in life, or at least as I remembered him. When I knew him, Dan had sported piercings in nearly every spot possible, but I didn't see any evidence of them now. He was dressed in a suit and tie. It looked wrong on him.

Diane was surprised. "He had more piercings than me. Where'd they go?"

"I don't know. Maybe his parents didn't approve."

"Hmph. They do look like staunch conservatives." Diane linked her arm through mine. "Let's get out of this room. These flowers are making my nose run."

Shortly, everyone filed outside and stood somberly as the casket was carried out. The ceremony was brief; the standard ashes-to-ashes spiel. Oddly, there was no mention of Dan's military service. Diane and I were heading for the parking lot when someone called to us.

"Excuse me." It was the man in the expensive suit. Expensive shoes, tie, everything. Including, unfortunately, strong cologne. Drakkar Noir: one of the worst offenders when it came to my lungs. I tried not to breathe deeply.

"I overheard you introducing yourselves to the family." He smiled thinly, but his gaze was belligerent. "I thought I knew all of Dan's friends. I'm Benjamin Goldstein. Dan's lover."

An odd choice of words these days. Did he want to shock us? I said, "We're so sorry for your loss. We were in library school with Dan."

"Ah." Goldstein surveyed both of us and didn't seem impressed. "You're not medical librarians."

"No." What an ass. "Are you?" I could do belligerent too.

Goldstein snorted. "I'm on the clinical faculty at USC School of Medicine."

A doctor. No wonder. Suddenly it hit me. Benjamin Goldstein. The authors of the second article were Oliver, Wray and Goldstein. B. Goldstein. *Holy shit*. The picture was suddenly a lot more complicated.

"Oh, how wonderful." Diane stepped in as I tried to control my facial expressions. "Were you close to Dan's family?"

"God, no." Goldstein's face twisted with disgust. "Pathetic, right-wing losers. Their precious son couldn't be gay, no matter what he said. They never accepted him for who he was. We'd been together for nearly two years, and this is the first time I ever saw them. He'd cut ties with them almost completely, but as soon as he was gone they swooped in and took control of everything. If they'd known who I was, I'm sure they would have had me removed."

That could explain the belligerence. I stood up straighter and looked right at Goldstein. "I'd like to have seen them try."

Goldstein looked at me in surprise, then barked a short laugh. "I wish they had. Dan would have loved it." He shook his head. "I have to go. Thanks for coming." He turned and strode away.

Diane watched him go, then turned to me. "Well. I don't even know what to say about that. Want to get a cup of coffee?"

"I'd better not." I hadn't been paying attention, but now I realized that I was short of breath. "I need to get back into air conditioning. You can owe me one."

"Okay, rain check it is." Diane patted me on the arm. "Let's get you back to safety."

On the way back to campus, I tried to sort out what I knew. I'd now met two of the three authors of the second article. Benjamin Goldstein seemed to be grieving over Dan, but did he know Dan was questioning the article he wrote? I only had Goldstein's word that he and Dan were still together. Had Dan confronted him with some kind of evidence? If they were still together, why would Dan be investigating his boyfriend's work?

Then there was Dr. Oliver. He seemed awfully paranoid about the possibility that someone would copy his research. Would he be willing to kill someone to protect it? Surely not. He seemed the type who would rather bankrupt a patent infringer in court.

None of it made sense. And I still didn't know if there was anything unusual at all about Dan's death, much less a murder. I needed to ask Kevin to check on the autopsy report.

The smog, flowers, and cologne had done a number on me. I used my inhaler in the car, but it wasn't helping as much as I'd like. By the time we got back to Westwood, it was nearly 4:30. I picked up my laptop from my office, and called Dr. Loomis to tell her I'd finish out the day working from home.

When I got home, though, it occurred to me that there was something better to do. I could go to Cedars and see if I could get a look in Dan's office. Maybe he'd left something there that would give me a clue or two about how to solve this puzzle he'd dumped in my lap.

Because I *was* going to solve this.

I turned around and went out to my car.

The parking lot at Cedars was nearly full. I got a spot near the street but far from the hospital door. I went into the lobby and checked the directory, then headed for the stairs.

I walked into the library and looked around. It was a small space, with books on one wall, journals on two walls, and computers in the center. There was a reception desk, but no one was there. There was a door in the far wall, with Dan's name posted on it. I tried the handle; it was unlocked.

I eased into Dan's office, leaving the door open. If anyone showed up, I could claim that I was looking for someone to help me. Dan's office was small, much smaller than mine, and crammed full: books, journals, scattered computer equipment, and too many chairs for the space. His desk was so close to the back wall that it was hard to see how a person could slide into the chair behind it. I was going to try, though.

I squeezed behind the desk and looked around. I doubted that Dan would have left anything lying around in the open, but I scanned the items on the surface of his desk just to make sure. There was a textbook to the right - *Essentials of Stem Cell Biology*. So he was reading up on the subject. He could have passed that off as being interested in Ben's work without raising suspicion.

I slid open the drawer to my right. It held an unorganized mashup of office supplies. The drawer to my left contained a stack of printer paper. The drawer in the center was locked. I got up and checked out in the hallway; no one was in sight. I went back to the desk, pulled a paper clip out of the jumble of office supplies, picked the lock on the center drawer, and found what I was looking for.

Inside the drawer were two items. One was a 5x7 picture of Dan with Ben. They seemed to be on a tropical island. They were holding frozen drinks with umbrellas in them and had their arms around each other. They looked happy. Dan's piercings were nowhere to be seen. Apparently he'd made a few changes in his life.

So Dan was out at work, but Ben wasn't? I couldn't think of any other reason for Dan to be hiding the picture. Ben hadn't hesitated to mention his relationship with Dan at the funeral. But if Ben was out and proud at work, I thought Dan would have displayed the photo. Or - maybe he and Ben had split, but Dan still had feelings for Ben and had kept the picture.

The other thing in the drawer was a manila folder. I slid it out of the drawer into my lap and closed the drawer quietly. Inside the file folder was a copy of Oliver's article. There were several places throughout it where Dan had underlined passages. He'd made cryptic notes to himself in places - "Medium?" "SEM?" "Source?" but I didn't understand them. There was one I understood, written at the beginning of the statistical section: "BULLSHIT!"

Nothing cryptic about that.

I folded the article into thirds and slid it into my inner jacket pocket. I put the file folder back where I found it and was closing the drawer when a voice said, "Hey! What are you doing in there?"

I jumped to my feet, whacking my right kneecap on the bottom of the drawer. *Ow*. A very young woman was standing at the reception desk, staring at me. "Who are you? I'm going to call security!"

"No, no, please don't do that." I came out of Dan's office but didn't move any closer to the girl, who looked more scared than angry. "I'm a friend of Dan's, and I just came from his funeral, and I just..." I tried to look very, very sad. "I wanted to see - where it happened, you know?"

Her expression softened, but she was still suspicious. "Are you on staff here? I've never seen you."

"No. I work at UCLA. I'm Dr. Jamie Brodie." If she thought I was a medical doctor, I wasn't going to correct her impression. "Do you want to see my ID?"

"Yes, please."

I pulled out my UCLA employee badge. She examined it for a minute then handed it back. "I'm Lily. Mr. Christensen was my boss." She sat at the reception desk and looked up at me. "I wanted to go to the funeral, but since I'm the only other employee in the library, I couldn't go. Was it nice?"

Not really. "It was outdoors, so that was nice."

She nodded. "He would have liked that. So, this is like a pilgrimage for you? I understand completely."

"Yes, exactly." I relaxed. It seemed that Lily was just gullible enough to let me get away with this. "How long did you work for Dan?"

"Only about six months. I liked working for him. He wasn't demanding at all." She looked at me sympathetically. "I hope you don't think this is too forward, but... Were you one of his boyfriends?"

Wow. So Dan *had* been out here, at least a little bit. "Yes, I was, several years ago. I hadn't seen him for a while. I was so shocked when he died."

She nodded. "We all were. Did you know he had seizures?"

"I did."

"No one here knew. But the police went to his house and found the anti-seizure medication." Her face took on a slightly disapproving expression. "He didn't share much."

"But he was out here."

She looked puzzled. "Out? Oh, out of the closet! Yes, he was. He didn't hide that at all. You could really say that he flaunted it some. He wore his rainbow pin all the time, and just the way he talked and dressed and did his hair - it was pretty obvious."

That was a major change from when I'd known Dan. "Did that bother people here?"

"Not me, not at all." Lily crossed her arms and looked defiant. "But it bothered some of the doctors, especially the older ones. And some of the older nurses too, and some of the male nurses..." She paused and made a face. "I guess it bothered a lot of people. But there were a lot of people that were fine with it too."

I nodded, thinking. Even if Dan's death wasn't accidental, maybe it didn't have anything to do with the letter. Maybe he was facing a different kind of enemy. "I'm glad he wasn't hiding it." I smiled at her, still trying to look sad. It wasn't hard; this *was* sad. "Thank you for letting me be in here for a while. It's made me feel better."

She smiled. "Oh, good. I'm glad I could help."

"I wonder if you could do one thing for me. Or, rather, not do something." I leaned in, conspiratorially. "Please don't mention to anyone that I was here. I wouldn't want it to get back to Dan's current boyfriend that I'd been here."

She looked surprised. "Okay. I don't think Dr. Goldstein would mind, but I won't tell him."

So they were together, and at least one other person knew it. Interesting. "Thanks, Lily. I appreciate that." If there was something to Dan's paranoia, maybe the person or persons responsible wouldn't find out that I'd been here.

But when I got to my car, all four tires had been slashed.

I said a few choice words and looked around. None of the other cars nearby had been damaged. Just mine. Should I report it? Yes, I should. I called Kevin. After he read me the riot act for staying out on a bad air day, he said he'd inform the appropriate station.

In about thirty minutes, a patrol car from Wilshire Division arrived. The officer took a look and shook his head. "We'll dust for prints, in case they touched your fenders while they were doing the slashing, but the chances of finding out who did it are pretty slim. This area isn't covered by cameras."

I shrugged. "I knew it was a long shot, but I figured you all would rather know than not."

"You're right. If we do find some evidence, or if it happens again, then the detectives can look into it further."

The evidence techs arrived in a few minutes and did raise a couple of palm prints. Maybe they would be able to find something out. I signed off on the police report, and the officer gave me a copy of it for my insurance. He left, and I called Triple A.

Kevin and the tow truck arrived about the same time. I filled Kevin in on the events of the day as the wrecker winched up my car. The tow truck headed to the garage with my VW, and I got in Kevin's car to go home.

Kevin started the engine, then turned and looked at me. "So. Your computer is messed up, and it's the only one that is, and your tires are slashed, and they're the only ones that are. Think there's any connection?"

"It's unusual, but I still don't see how there could be a link. Computers crash all the time. It just so happened that this was my week for it. And the tires - who knows? *No one* knew I was coming here. I didn't even know I was coming here. Maybe someone didn't like my 'No to Prop 8' bumper sticker."

"Maybe." Kevin started the car. "But I don't like coincidences. I'll check on those palm prints, see if anything turns up."

"Gee, thanks, detective." I stuck my tongue out at him.

He laughed. "Hey, we protect *and* serve."

Since we had a car, we stopped at the grocery store. By the time we got home I was getting tired. It was Abby's turn to make dinner, and she had soup and sandwiches ready. After dinner, Kevin and Abby settled in to watch TV, and I started reading the second article again. The methodology was hard to follow, and the statistics were beyond me, but the results were pretty clear. Their procedure had been successful. The discussion noted the possible application to fertility treatment. It was couched in scientific language, but reading between the lines, I thought the authors sounded pretty pleased with themselves. That would certainly fit with my initial impression of both of the authors I'd met.

I retrieved the copy of the article that I'd found in Dan's desk and studied his margin notes again. I Googled "SEM" and found that it stood for scanning electron microscopy. "Source" probably meant just that – Dan was wondering about the source for the statement. "Medium" was still a mystery. I looked again at his "BULLSHIT" notation over the statistics section. I was going to have to take a shot at interpreting those. But I'd have to do that at some time other than late evening. My brain wasn't up to it now.

Before I went to bed, I used my peak flowmeter to check my lung function. I was supposed to check and record it every morning and evening, but sometimes I forgot. I'd been trying to be more consistent with it since I got out of the hospital. This morning my peak flow had been within 90% of normal, but this evening it had dropped, to 82%. If it got below 80%, I was supposed to call the doctor.

I decided to take a hot shower before bed. I needed that peak flow to come back up by morning. Fifteen minutes of breathing clean, steamy air should get it turned around.

I still wasn't much closer to figuring out anything about Dan's request. Tomorrow was Friday. In the morning I had my budget presentation, but after that, maybe I could find someone to help me analyze the statistical section of Oliver's article. Or at least find a copy of "Statistics for Dummies."

I thought about my impressions of Drs. Oliver and Goldstein. The first thing I'd noticed with both of them was how expensively they were dressed. Did stem cell research pay that well? And how did they make their money? I needed to do a little research of my own, into the authors of the two articles and the labs they worked in.

Chapter 4
Friday, June 1

The next morning, I hit the snooze button three times before I could drag my brain to full consciousness. God, I was tired. I sat up and checked my lung function before I even got out of bed. It was at 84% - still not good, but slightly better than yesterday. I'd have to be extra careful today.

I used my daily inhaler, took a steamy shower, and felt better. When I went to the kitchen Abby was there, pouring coffee into her gargantuan travel mug. "How are you feeling? I heard you coughing last night."

I was coughing in my sleep? That was bad news. "I'm okay. I was outside too much yesterday. My tires got slashed, and I had to wait for Triple A."

"Yeah, Kev mentioned that."

I poured cereal in a bowl and took the milk from the fridge. "Is he gone already?"

"Yep. Yesterday and today. Seems we're having a murder wave in West LA." She walked past me to the door, patting me on the head. I swatted at her hand. She picked up her tool belt. "Stay inside. Take care of yourself today."

"Yes, Mom." I stuck my tongue out at her. She laughed and closed the door. I finished my cereal and went to work.

I opened my office door onto a disaster. The mess I'd returned to on Tuesday was nothing compared to this. The whole place was tossed. My file cabinets had been locked, but they'd managed to break into the file cabinet drawers and dump everything out. The floor and all of the furniture was coated in at least two inches of paper. All the books had been dumped off the shelves.

A quick survey didn't show that anything was missing. Hell, it looked like they'd *added* stuff to what was already in here. My diplomas were still hanging from the walls, and my pictures were still intact in their frames on the tops of my bookshelves. Everything else, though, was on the floor.

And when I turned on my computer, I got the blue screen again.

Fan-fucking-tastic.

I called IT and left another message. This was ridiculous. When IT Andy or whoever got here, I was going to ask them to replace the computer. It must have gotten a virus of some sort which caused the email fiasco and then wiped the hard drive again. I didn't understand how that was possible, but it had happened, so it *must* be possible.

It occurred to me again that I'd found Diane behind my desk twice this week. When she picked me up yesterday she was supposed to meet me outside, but she'd made a point to get here early and come to my office. I'd only been in the men's room a couple of minutes. Why would she need to check her email then? And didn't she have a smart phone? Yes, she did; she'd pulled it out and checked it after the funeral.

But *why* would Diane mess with my computer? Was that her idea of a joke?

She'd kept in touch with Dan; did she have some knowledge about what he was investigating?

No. Diane couldn't be involved in this. There *must* be some innocent explanation for her actions.

But she was the only other person that had used my computer. Whoever broke in to the office last night wouldn't have been able to log on.

I'd have to figure out a way to ask her about it that didn't sound accusatory.

And if Diane wasn't sabotaging my computer, who was? And why?

All of the weirdness had started after I got Dan's letter.

I sat down and took out a pen, found a scrap of paper, and started making a list.

1. Tuesday - Diane comes in, I find her behind my desk
2. Dan's letter - someone after him?
3. Wednesday - Dr. Oliver shows up after I request his article
4. Wednesday, computer dead
5. Creepy feeling Wednesday night – being watched?
6. Thursday morning, email hacked
7. Diane comes in, catch her using computer
8. Thursday at funeral, author #2, Dan's boyfriend, acting funny?
9. Thursday evening, tires slashed
10. Today, office broken into
11. Today, computer dead again

Wow. I hadn't realized the list of weirdness had grown to eleven items. That was a shitload of coincidence.

A thought occurred to me. At one of our safety updates from the UCLA Police Department last fall, they talked about having a detective that investigated computer crimes. Would this computer problem of mine qualify as something worthy of investigation?

One way to find out. I called the police department main number and was transferred to the computer crimes detective. He wasn't in; I left a voicemail with a brief explanation and asked him to call me back.

Then I called back to the main number and reported that my office had been broken into. *Duh.* The dispatcher said he'd have someone right there.

A few minutes later, an officer named Antonio Jenkins appeared at my door. He surveyed the mess, took my statement, and called forensics. They arrived and started lifting fingerprints. Most of them would naturally be mine, which were already on file from my initial employment background check. I told Officer Jenkins about my computer issues, and he said I'd done the right thing by calling the computer crimes detective. He didn't have an opinion about whether or not the detective would investigate my computer.

Officer Jenkins finished and left. I needed to clean up, but it was going to have to wait. My budget meeting was happening in less than 20 minutes.

I hoped the detective would return my call before IT got here. If I turned my computer over to the police, IT would be forced to give me a new one.

And if the police could tell me what had been done to my computer, I could then decide whether I should speak to Diane about it.

The budget meeting was relatively painless, and my presentation was well received. It was a relief to have that behind me. When I got back to my office, the computer crimes detective was waiting for me.

I introduced myself. "I'm surprised to see you in person. Thanks for coming over."

"No problem." Roger Blake was tall, thin, and weathered. He reminded me of a hawk – an intense, beady-eyed predator. He had a pack of cigarettes in his jacket pocket and was chewing gum vigorously. "I hadn't been in this building in a long time. Figured I'd take a field trip." The mess in my office took him aback. "Whoa. What happened here?"

I shoved a pile of papers off the chair, invited him to sit, and told him about the break-in. He listened, drumming his fingers on the arm of the chair. "Interesting. Okay, tell me about your computer problems."

I described everything that had happened - the daily issues with crashes and email and internet access and finding Diane behind my desk twice. Blake listened, then got out pen and paper and asked me to repeat everything, in detail, with dates and times. When I finished, he sat back and steepled his fingers. "And you're the only one in the library that has had any problems."

"Yes, sir. Which makes me think it must be directed at me, but I have no idea who's doing it or why it's happening."

"What makes you think it's not this DeLong woman?"

"Because she has no reason to do anything like this, and I'm not sure she has the skills. And she couldn't have been the one to come in and trash my office last night."

"She's not UCLA personnel?"

"No, sir. She's on staff at Pasadena High School."

"She live in Pasadena?"

"No, sir. West Hollywood."

"Hmph." West Hollywood didn't meet with Blake's approval. "Okay. Think back. Last Wednesday. Before your computer crashed for the first time. What happened that day?"

"It was my second day back at work. I'd been out for two weeks after a bad asthma attack. Everything was fine on Tuesday. Everything was fine when I came in on Wednesday. I worked in my office in the morning, then I went to the biomedical library to request a couple of articles from their databases. Then I had a meeting in the education building. When I got back from my meeting, my computer had crashed. That was the first time."

Blake looked puzzled. "None of that sounds particularly ominous. Is all of that routine for you?"

"For the most part."

His eyes narrowed a bit. "What do you mean, the most part?"

"Well, it's not every day that I go to the biomedical library. I hardly ever go there at all. I'm a history librarian."

"Why did you go there that day?"

He was closing in on my own suspicions. I pulled out Dan's letter and handed it to him. "Last Tuesday morning, I found out that my friend, Dan Christensen, had died over the weekend. It was a surprise because he was young, only 37. Then, last Tuesday afternoon, I found this letter from him in the mail. It was these two articles that I requested from the biomed library."

"Can I make a copy of this?"

"Sure."

Blake left the office for a second, came back with his copy of Dan's letter and handed the original back to me. "What did you think when you got this?"

"I was kind of freaked out. He says right there, 'If anything happens to me,' and something had happened to him."

"Did they give a cause of death?"

"Not yet. My brother is a detective with LAPD. He'll get the autopsy report when it's released, but it's too soon. You know how that goes."

"I sure do. I was with LAPD for 15 years. Are they investigating this as a homicide?"

"No, sir. They're not investigating it at all."

"Hmm." Blake tapped the edge of the copied letter on the arm of the chair, thinking. "So if your buddy was involved in something weird... Could your request of the articles have triggered something? Pointed someone out there in your direction?"

"It did point Dr. Oliver in my direction. But he seemed harmless, and satisfied with my explanation about why I wanted his article."

"Huh." Blake reached into his pocket and pulled out a pack of gum. Dentyne. He stuffed two more sticks into his mouth. I wondered how many he already had in there.

"You're a librarian. You know about electronic databases."

"Yes, sir."

"So you know that it's possible to create alerts. If an article gets published on a particular subject, you get an email alert, and you can retrieve the article from the database."

"Right."

"So this Oliver guy has an alert set up to notify him when someone downloads his article. Maybe he's not the only one who did that. What do you know about the other authors?"

"Nothing. I did meet one of the other authors at Dan's funeral. He said he was Dan's boyfriend. He didn't say anything about articles."

Blake was chomping away on his gum. Maybe it helped him think. "Boyfriend, huh? You think this is some kind of weird gay thing?"

Oh brother. "No."

"Hmph." Blake sounded like he was going to reserve judgment on that point for now. Probably conjuring up a gang of murderous gay hackers based in West Hollywood. He looked back at the titles in Dan's letter. "Stem cell research, huh?"

"Yeah. I've read the second one, but I'm waiting for the first one to come through interlibrary loan."

"What language is that?"

"Welsh."

"Bizarre. And so far, nothing has turned up in the article that seems worthy of instigating computer sabotage?"

"Not at all. And the authors of the article aren't affiliated with UCLA. They're at Cedars and they're on clinical faculty at USC."

"Okay." Another stick of Dentyne disappeared into Blake's jaw. Where was he putting it all? "Tell me more about Ms. DeLong."

"She was in library school with me and Dan. The guy who died. She's the librarian at Pasadena High. She's…" I realized I didn't really know all that much about Diane. "She's a friend." That sounded lame even to me.

Blake drummed his fingers on the chair for a minute. "Okay, here's what we'll do. I'm going to take your computer with me and see what's been done to it, and I'll have a chat with your friend, Ms. DeLong. In the meantime, can you switch the computers you use every day?"

"Yeah. It'll be inconvenient, but I can do it."

"Good." Blake slapped his knees and stood up. "Let's get this thing taken apart."

I borrowed a book cart from the East Asian Library around the corner. I heaved the computer tower onto the cart, and we unhooked everything. Blake pushed the cart into the hallway. "I'll let you know what I find."

"Thank you."

Finally, I had time to start repairing the mess that the burglar had made. First, I created a pile with the loose papers and file folders. I'd address those at some other time. I was kicking up a lot of dust, and I didn't want to start wheezing. But I did want to get the books re-shelved – the natural obsessive-compulsive tendencies of a librarian to organize books taking over. When I finished I took a puff from the inhaler that I kept in my desk drawer. It was getting low; I'd have to bring a replacement next week.

It was time for my reference shift. Right on time, Clinton appeared at the reference desk. We weren't busy at that moment, and he walked right up to me.

"Hi, Clinton."

He looked at me gravely. "The word of the day is *chrestomathy.*"

I had to ask him how to spell that one. Liz wrote it in the log; he bowed and walked away. I looked it up. It meant *a collection of selected literary passages.*

Not sure I could use that one in a sentence by the end of the day.

Back in my office I did a quick Google check for the authors of both of the articles. The Americans were easy to find. Tristan Oliver, MD, PhD, and Alana Wray, MD, were the medical directors of Fertility Research. Benjamin Goldstein, MD, was apparently their employee. Fertility Research seemed to be a small, privately-funded organization, renting space in one of the medical office buildings adjacent to Cedars. Its website wasn't very informative, but it did include the doctors' credentials and a list of their publications.

Oliver, Wray, and Goldstein were graduates of US medical schools. Oliver had done a stint at Cambridge University, doing post-fellowship work in stem cell research back in 2002-3. Then he'd come to LA and joined forces with Wray, who had done postdoctoral training at NIH. They applied for a grant to open their own lab; a year after that, they'd published their first of many articles. The 2007 article that I now had was their big breakthrough. Both doctors were listed as clinical faculty at USC's medical school, but I couldn't find any evidence that they actually taught anything. Maybe they taught stem cell research. Goldstein, for his part, had co-written articles with Wray and Oliver since the 2007 paper, but hadn't gone to work for the lab until 2010, when he'd finished his OB-GYN residency at USC.

After the publication of the 2007 article, Oliver and Wray's lab had no difficulties in getting funded. At least every other month, Oliver was pictured accepting a very large check from a "sponsor." Oliver's name was in the "Living" section of the LA Times a couple of times a year. He and his wife hosted fundraisers at their Bel-Air home for various charities. Everyone looked tastefully wealthy. Wray's name turned up more often in the results of West Coast triathlons, often finishing in the top three in her age group, 40-45. One article had a blurry picture of her crossing a finish line, but her face was covered with a ball cap and it wasn't possible to tell what she looked like. There was a feature article from 2009 on the lab itself; Oliver was pictured, and Wray spoke movingly about her lifelong quest for better answers to the problem of infertility.

Benjamin Goldstein didn't turn up in any news at all other than his appointment to the lab.

The Welsh authors were a different story. David Hughes and Marc Llewellyn had been researchers at a similar lab at Oxford until mid-2003. They had also published a series of papers, but none of them were breakthroughs. The papers had been published in decreasingly prestigious journals, until their last article, the one cited by Dan in his letter, had appeared in the Welsh Medical Journal. The funding for the lab dried up, and it was closed. Neither man had ever published again.

Interestingly, the existence of Hughes and Llewellyn's lab overlapped in time with Tristan Oliver's years at Cambridge. Oliver might have known Hughes and Llewellyn. It wasn't unusual for researchers with a narrow specialty to be professionally incestuous. Everyone in a unique subspecialty knew everyone else, whether it was Celtic warrior queen Boudicca - the subject of my doctoral dissertation - or stem cell fertility research.

The most surprising information about Hughes and Llewellyn was that they were both dead. David Hughes had died in 2006 of a heart attack while on his morning jog. He had been in his 60s. Marc Llewellyn had died in 2003, not long after the publication of his last article, in a horrific car crash on the M40 outside Oxford. I flinched involuntarily; I'd been on that stretch of road many times. The accident had been a hit-and-run; one car, driven by Llewellyn, had been nearly destroyed. The other was never found, and there were no witnesses, so the investigation had gone nowhere. Llewellyn wasn't killed outright, but suffered severe head trauma and passed away the next day.

I considered what I had learned. Two articles, three dead men. Was it just bad luck? It didn't seem to be bad luck for Oliver et al. They were doing just fine. Hughes's death seemed ordinary enough, and on the surface, so did Dan's. Llewellyn's car accident was likely just a case of being in the wrong place at the wrong time.

The article titles made more sense now. It was as I'd originally thought. Hughes and Llewellyn hadn't been successful with their research, so they'd published their last article and given it up. Oliver had probably become aware of Hughes and Llewellyn's work when he was in Cambridge, and had come back to the U.S. to continue the research in his own lab. A few years later, with better technology, Oliver and Wray figured out how to make it work and published their article. The breakthrough had brought the money pouring in, and the doctors were now reaping the rewards of their hard work. And Oliver and Wray had probably hired Benjamin Goldstein to give themselves more time away from the lab to raise money and host parties and compete in triathlons.

It all made perfect sense, except for one thing.

What had Dan wanted me to find out?

It was time to go home, and I still hadn't done anything with the statistics in Oliver and Wray's article. Maybe I'd work on that over the weekend. I still didn't have the Welsh article, so there wasn't anything else I could accomplish until I got it. I decided to go home.

I was dragging as I walked across campus. What a week. It was only four days, and it felt like forty. I was exhausted.

There weren't a lot of people around, even though it was early evening and still fully light. As I passed the intramural fields, it registered that someone was behind me. I didn't think much of it until I crossed Gayley and the guy was still with me. I could tell it was a guy, but I couldn't see anything that would allow me to describe him in any more detail. He was wearing a ball cap, hoodie, and jeans. Just like 95% of the male students at the university.

I turned onto Landfair from Strathmore and headed south. My apartment was on Roebling, but if I was being followed, I didn't want to lead the guy straight to it. I was considering passing up Roebling and crossing back onto campus when I got to the end of Landfair. I'd just about decided to do that when the guy turned off, into an apartment complex about three buildings up from Roebling.

Now who was paranoid? I chastised myself and promptly forgot all about it.

Chapter 5
Saturday, June 2

Saturday morning dawned with the promise of a beautiful day. Pete and Kevin had planned a day of hiking in Topanga Canyon, and I had decided to go along. Abby was going too, and my brother Jeff was taking a rare Saturday off to come with us.

Jeff was the oldest, a year older than Kevin and two years older than me. He was a veterinarian, and lived in Oceanside, the town where we'd grown up, with his wife Valerie and their two boys. He'd run cross country in high school and college and was still wiry. He'd stopped running to save his knees, but he still surfed and took the boys hiking at every opportunity. And, occasionally, he'd drive up the coast and join us on the trails for a day.

Jeff showed up at the apartment at the crack of dawn. I had just smacked the snooze button for the second time when I heard pounding on the door. I pulled on a pair of sweats and staggered into the living room. I could hear the shower running. It was probably Abby; she was one of *those* people. Morning people. I opened the door. "Good Lord. What time did you get up?"

"4:30. And I drove fast." Jeff gave me a hug. "How ya doin'?"

"Fine. How's everything at home?"

"Fine. Colin's decided he wants to go to space camp this summer, so we need to find one. Is there anything at Cal Tech?"

"I don't know, but I can find out."

"Would you? And let me know. We'd rather not send him out of state at age ten."

"Right." I scratched a note to myself on the refrigerator message board.

Kevin appeared, and the talk devolved into brotherly insults. Abby yelled out the door for us to shut up and load the car. So we did.

We all piled into Jeff's CR-V and drove to Santa Monica to pick up Pete.

Pete lived in Santa Monica on 17th Street, just around the corner from Wilshire, in a townhouse he'd inherited from a great-uncle. The place was beautiful, and the location was great. Pete could walk to his teaching job at Santa Monica College and jog to the beach.

When we pulled up, I jumped out of the passenger seat and went to the door. Pete was ready, meeting me at the door with his backpack in hand. He grinned and gave me a quick hug, which was a little surprising, but I hugged him back. "Come on, you get the front seat."

He laughed. "It pays to be the tallest."

"Ha ha." I lifted his backpack as he locked the door. "Holy shit, what do you have in here? Bricks?"

"Nah, concrete blocks today." He took it from me and did a couple of biceps curls with it. "It's not that heavy, you wuss."

"I'll show you wuss." I chased him down the sidewalk, where we proceeded to let Jeff and Kevin join in the teasing and friendly insults all the way to Topanga Canyon. By the time we got there, Abby was threatening to walk back home.

We found a parking spot without too much trouble, since we were so early, and headed toward Eagle Rock. We were chatting along the way when we spotted a dead field mouse at the side of the trail. Jeff commented on it, and Kevin said, "Oh, that reminds me, I got the autopsy results on your friend last night."

Pete said, "Wow, that was fast."

Jeff said, "What friend?"

I said, "What did it show?"

"Not much." Kevin took a drink of water. "There wasn't anything inconsistent with a seizure, except that there were therapeutic levels of his seizure medication in his blood. But that doesn't mean he didn't have a seizure. It was too long from the time of death to determine whether his muscle enzymes were elevated, like they would have been immediately after the seizure."

"But the fact that the levels of his meds were where they should be - isn't that a little odd? Did the coroner comment on it?"

"He commented on it to the extent that he said it was a little odd. That was it. There was nothing else to suggest any other cause of death. There was nothing at all to suggest foul play. So the coroner signed it off as probable seizure. He didn't have anything else to hang it on."

Jeff held up his hand. "Okay. Somebody tell me what's going on."

I told everything, right through my silly thought that I might have been followed last night. Kevin was interested to hear what the computer crimes detective had said yesterday.

When I finished, Jeff said, "Okay, let's recap. Your buddy dies under what the coroner refers to as 'odd' circumstances. Then you get a letter from said buddy, suggesting that he's in danger of some sort and passing his investigation of these two articles on to you. Then you request said articles and weird shit starts happening to you. Your computer goes wonky three days in a row, one of the doctors shows up in person to question you, another of the doctors shows up at the funeral and turns out to be your dead buddy's boyfriend, you visit the scene of the death and your tires get slashed, and then someone follows you home last night. All of that sounds pretty suspicious to me."

"But there are alternate explanations of everything so far." Pete started ticking off on his fingers. "There's no evidence that Dan didn't die of a seizure. You said he'd had a head injury and had some emotional problems as a result; his paranoia could be explained that way. You saw your friend Diane using your computer; she could be punking you for some reason. The doctor that visited you said that he was worried about patent infringement. The doctor at the funeral had reason to be there, assuming he really was the boyfriend. You said yourself that your tires might have been slashed because of your Prop 8 bumper sticker. And you also said yourself that the guy following you turned off well before you did, and you had decided he wasn't following you after all. Although..." He folded the fingers he'd been counting on into a fist. "The circumstantial evidence for *something* going on is starting to pile up."

Kevin said, "But it is circumstantial. There's no solid evidence of anything yet."

Abby said, "But there may be, after the UCLA cops finish with your computer."

I said, "Yeah, and I'm afraid that will show that Diane was responsible."

Jeff said, "Have you found anything in the articles yet to explain what Dan might have been getting at?"

"No. Although, on the copy of the article I found in his desk, he had written BULLSHIT in capital letters over the top of the statistics section. I need to figure out what the statistics show and why he might have written that."

"I might be able to help you with that." Pete glanced at me as he picked his way around a couple of rocks. "I did recently finish a dissertation for which I had to do a lot of stats. It's moderately fresh in my mind."

"That would be great. I was going to try to figure it out with help from the Internet, but I'm sure it won't take as long for you."

He laughed. "Well, I wouldn't be too sure about that, but I'll do my best."

We were back home by mid-afternoon after dropping Pete off. Jeff needed to start for home, and I was tired again. Kevin and Abby left to go to Abby's sister's for a cookout. Abby had invited me, but I begged off. I'd spent my evenings reading this stupid medical article, and I was getting behind on my other reading. I had a new issue of the Journal of Scottish Historical Studies and a stack of books that were calling to me. I propped pillows behind me on the sofa, and settled in for an evening of reading.

I had dozed off with a book propped on my chest when a sound woke me.

I didn't move, listening to see if I heard it again. There was nothing for several seconds. Then I heard it again, a soft scratching sound, coming from our balcony.

We lived on the fourth floor of our building. It was dark out, but our balcony, like all the others at the complex, overlooked the small courtyard, if you could even call it that. Theoretically, no one should have been able to climb up without being seen.

I heard the sound again. I turned off the light behind my head, let my eyes adjust, and waited to see if I heard it again.

There it was.

I eased off the sofa as silently as possible. We had vertical blinds covering the sliding glass door. The blinds were closed, and I knew the door was locked because no one had been out there since we got home from the mountains.

We had two doors to the main balcony, the one in the living room and the one in my bedroom. There was a second, private balcony outside Kevin's room. I went there, slid the blinds open, and looked out the door. I still couldn't see anything. Kevin's service weapon was locked in a safe, and I didn't want to take the time to open it. I picked up the baseball bat that Kevin had propped in the corner of his room. I moved the bar that prevented the door from being opened, unlocked the door as quietly as I could, and stepped out onto the balcony.

I had to look around the corner from Kevin's balcony to the main one. There was a figure crouched at the base of the door that led into my bedroom.

I eased back into Kevin's bedroom, slid the door closed as silently as possible, got the phone from the bedside table, and dialed 911.

"911, what is your emergency?"

"There's someone trying to break in my apartment."

The dispatcher read off my address then asked for my apartment number and the details of what was happening. She kept me on the line until I saw the reflection of flashing lights in the parking lot, then hung up. I went to the door and let the officer in. His partner and another pair of officers were on the ground below our balcony. The officer in the apartment went to Kevin's balcony and looked around.

The guy was gone.

The officer holstered his gun, which he had pulled out when entering Kevin's bedroom. "He probably got scared off when he saw our lights. We'll search on foot down there." He went into my bedroom, opened the blinds and the door, and stepped out. "Yep, here we go. He was trying to use this cutting tool." He held up a thing that looked like a protractor from high school geometry and pointed to a set of circular scratches beside the door handle. "It still wouldn't have gotten him in because the bar is in place, but it would have gotten him started." He called for forensics. "We'll have the evidence guys come and see if they can pull up anything. You never know. Maybe he's not a very bright burglar." He pointed at the baseball bat, which I was still clutching. "You know how to use that thing?"

"Yes, sir. I was a Little League home run champion."

"Where'd you play?"

"Oceanside."

He looked puzzled. "I'm from eastern Oregon. Where's Oceanside?"

"Just north of San Diego, just south of Camp Pendleton."

"Ah." He looked around the apartment and spotted a picture of Jeff, Kevin, and me on the mantel. "Hey. That's Detective Brodie."

"Yeah. He's my roommate. And my brother."

"Oho." He looked back at me, appraising. "I can see the resemblance now. Where is he?"

"Out with his girlfriend. They probably went to the movies. Do you want me to call him?"

"Yeah, if you would."

I got my cell and called. Kevin and Abby had gone to the movies and were now in the car on the way home. Abby answered. I filled her in. She told Kevin what I was saying, and I heard him swearing in the background.

"We're on our way. Probably only five minutes." I heard more swearing. "Make that three minutes."

It was more like two and a half. Kevin, Abby and the forensics team all came through the front door at the same time. A small crowd had gathered now at the foot of the building, looking up at our balcony. The officers who were searching for the burglar weren't having any success. Kevin talked to the officer in the living room while I filled Abby in on all the details.

I was still hanging on to the baseball bat.

It took about another hour. Forensics finished up. The officers who were searching found nothing. Everyone said goodbye and cleared out. Kevin went around locking all the doors again and double checking everything. Then he turned to me.

I was still holding the baseball bat. He reached out for it. "I think you can let go of that now."

I handed it to him and flexed my fingers. My grip would probably be sore in the morning.

"That scared you some, huh?" Kevin got a beer out of the fridge and handed it to me.

"Yeah. It did."

He nodded. "Would have scared me too."

"No, it wouldn't. You'd have just shot the guy."

He laughed. "Well, not without getting some information out of him first." He got serious. "This convinces me that all of your incidents are related. Someone must be after you - if not to harm you personally, then at least to discourage you from doing whatever it is you're doing." He went into his bedroom with the baseball bat and returned with his current service weapon, a Glock 9mm, and an older model of the same gun that he'd started his career with. He handed me the older one and its clip. "Until this all gets straightened out, we keep these handy when we're home. Okay?"

"Yep." I'd learned to shoot as a kid; Master Gunnery Sgt. David Brodie, USMC, had made sure his offspring could handle weapons.

I didn't own one personally. I was starting to think that might need to change.

Chapter 6
Sunday, June 3

On Sunday, Kevin and Abby went for a drive up the coast with friends. I spent the morning doing chores. Around 10:30, I called Pete. He said he'd come over to look at the statistics section of the Oliver/Wray/Goldstein article, and bring lunch.

At noon, there was a knock on the door. I made sure it was Pete through the peephole, then opened the door. He handed me a big bag from In-N-Out. "What's with that sign in your elevator?"

"What sign?"

"The one that says, 'If the elevator stops, do not be alarmed, just push the alarm.' Somebody's being funny?"

"A little elevator humor, I guess."

"Yeah, very little."

"Oh, come on. That's a *little* funny."

"Okay, okay…"

We ate, then went to the living room. Pete had brought a book that he'd used as his stats bible when he was writing his dissertation. He set it to one side, got a notepad and pen, and started making notes while reading the statistics section of the article.

I just watched him. He was such a gorgeous guy. He glanced over at me once, saw me looking at him, and kind of gave me a sideways grin. I grinned back.

Twenty minutes later, he was finished. "It will be interesting to get the Welsh article, with the original procedure, to see if those authors used these same parameters to test for statistical significance. Because they've used some incredibly generous parameters."

"Okay - explain that to me."

"Look here." He showed me a chart. "Here's where they're measuring the number of cells that reacted the way they hoped, and this column is for the number of cells total. When you're running an experiment, it's not enough just to add up the results. You have to test for statistical significance."

"Statistical significance?"

"Yeah." He looked at me quizzically. "Didn't you have to take stats at Oxford? Or at least Berkeley?"

"I did at Berkeley, but that was fourteen years ago. And I didn't at Oxford."

"Really?"

"Really. Why would I? Historians don't do double-blind studies. We just dwell on the past."

Pete snorted. "Funny. Okay, then. The *p* value, here, is the test that's often used for statistical significance in this kind of trial. You can set the *p* value at whatever you like, but in general, the smaller it is, the better. The usual *p* values are either .05 or .01. If your experiment is statistically significant at *p* less than or equal to .01, then there's less than a 1% probability that your results were due to chance. These guys," he pointed at a number, "have used a *p* value of .25. That's awfully high."

"So their results aren't statistically significant?"

"There's still a 75% chance that their results were due to their experimental manipulations, and not due to chance. But I'm surprised that they got this published, with a *p* value at that level."

"Hm. You know, academic publishing is changing. There are a lot of second- and third-tier journals out there now that will take a paper that the top tier journals won't. I haven't looked at the specifics of this journal, whether it's even peer reviewed or not."

"Then maybe you should." Pete stood up. "I'm gonna get a beer. Want one?"

"Sure." I opened my laptop. Pete brought me an open bottle, and we clinked our bottles together. "Here's to research."

Pete laughed. "You're such a nerd."

"Yep. Out and proud, dude."

I got online and did a search for the Journal of Stem Cell Biology. Its website appeared. I swung the laptop around so Pete could see it too.

"The first thing to check is the publisher. And the publisher here is called..." I had to click in a couple of pages. "...Biology Journals Publishers. I've never heard of them, so it's not one of the big publishing houses. And - they're located in Sri Lanka. Not a good sign. Next question, is it peer reviewed?"

Pete pointed to the screen. "It says there that it is."

"Yeah, but just because they say it doesn't make it true. I need to look at the instructions for authors." I read through those. "See, it doesn't say anything about the author's submitted paper going through the peer review process. Which means it's extremely likely that the peer review process doesn't happen."

"Wow." Pete leaned back. "So almost anyone can start their own journal now and publish anything they want?"

"Yep." I clicked on the contents page for the current issue. "Look at this. Most of the articles are written by the same two guys in this issue. It looks to me like this primarily serves as a vanity publication for these guys, who happen to be the editors, with an occasional contribution from elsewhere."

"So how does a journal like that get indexed in a medical database?"

"It was in an obscure database, only available to the med school personnel. That's why I couldn't find the full text. If it had been in Medline or one of the other major medical databases, I could have printed it out myself."

Pete snorted softly. "And had Oliver at your doorstep even sooner than he was."

"True. So, Oliver comes back from Cambridge, and he and Wray want to open a lab. The profile I read said that they got a grant to get it started. I wonder if they're still getting grant money?"

"You could find out." Pete gestured to my laptop. "Federal grants have to be listed somewhere. It might take some digging."

"Yeah. But the grants also could be private. The newspaper story implied that they were privately funded now."

"Those grants might be hard to uncover. Although, if they were made from private, not-for-profit organizations, those organizations might list them."

I mused. "You know, the first thing that struck me about both Oliver and Ben Goldstein, when I met them, was how well they were dressed. They were both wearing Armani suits that run about two grand each, and thousand dollar shoes. That's when it occurred to me to check on their backgrounds because I couldn't believe that research paid that well."

Pete shrugged. "Maybe they have family money. Or married well."

"Maybe. Either way, if they opened the lab with a grant, they'd have to have something to show for the money if they were going to keep the grant or get new ones. And their procedure works, but it doesn't work as well as it should. So they get a paper published, in a journal of questionable reputation, which lets them report their results as successful with *p* values that are set too high."

Pete nodded. "If their grants are from private foundations that are sloppy about due diligence, then maybe all they need is a paper published in a supposedly peer-reviewed journal that says the procedure works. The foundations don't know any better, they just read the abstract, and they keep forking over the dough."

"So it's almost like they're running a scam."

"Yeah. Did you find anything to indicate whether they're treating patients or not?"

"No. I didn't get that impression." An idea occurred to me. "It might be instructive to pay a visit to the lab. Dr. Oliver told me to contact him if I had any more questions. So he wouldn't think anything about it if I did call him. I could look around, see if I can find any patients in the place."

"Whoa." Pete frowned. "That might not be safe."

"You could come with me."

Pete groaned. "No way. What excuse would you give for me being there?"

“Um - we could say that you were trying to decide whether to give to a foundation that supports stem cell research, and you wanted to see what kind of thing your money would be going to?”

Pete laughed. “I had no idea you were so devious.”

“Yeah, you did. That would work, right?”

“Sure. Whatever. If it’ll keep you from charging off by yourself. But we can’t tell Kevin.”

“Oh, God no. He’d toss us both off the balcony.”

Pete leaned back, crossed his arms, and gave me a stern look. “Now. I want to know how you knew those suits were Armani.”

I laughed. “Scott was into clothes. Everywhere we went, he’d point out what all the other men were wearing. I got so I could recognize brands pretty well. If we were out somewhere he’d actually quiz me.”

“Geez.” Pete looked at me critically. “That’s kind of shallow for your taste, isn’t it?”

“He had other good qualities. And, see, now that information has come in handy.”

“Okay, I’ll give him that.” Pete stood up. “Back to your case here. If we’re right, do you suppose what they’ve done constitutes fraud?”

“I don’t see how. It’s the fault of the granting agencies if they don’t do their due diligence. The information was there for them to find; if they didn’t look hard enough to find it, I don’t see how that would be fraudulent. Unethical, yes, but legally fraudulent? My guess would be no.”

Pete sighed. “I think you’re right.” He went to look out the sliding glass door. “But there’s no place in that scenario for the Welsh article. How does that fit?”

“I have no idea. And it’s hard for me to imagine Dan getting worked up about a breach of ethics on someone else’s part like this. Unless he was just trying to protect Ben. But in that case, why wouldn’t he just tell Ben? Ben could quietly look for another job, and that would be that.”

"Unless he thought Ben was involved."

"Yeah, we haven't ruled that out. And even if Dan was trying to protect Ben, that still doesn't explain the Welsh article. And why Dan would enlist me to keep investigating this."

Pete went to the kitchen and brought back two more beers. "Still some unanswered questions."

"Yep." I took a drink. "And I'm out of answers for now." I picked up the remote. "Want to watch a movie?"

We watched a movie, then an episode of "Hoarders" that was on the DVR. Kevin's ex was a hoarder; it was one of the reasons they'd split. He hated the show, but I was fascinated by it. After the show, Pete said, "God. Now I feel like going home and throwing everything away."

"I could understand it if they hoarded books. But it's almost never anything with value at all."

"But it's not about value, is it? With most of those people, it seems to be about security. And as I remember, that's what it was for Kevin's ex."

"How much more secure can you get than living with a cop?"

"Beats me. Neurosis is not my area of expertise. Psychosis, now, you're singing my song."

I yawned. "Speaking of psychosis, how's your textbook chapter coming?"

"There are a few more resources I have to check for updates, then I think I'll have all the research I need to start writing."

"Sounds like you need to spend more time at the library." I grinned.

"I do." Pete gave me a sideways look. "You telling me you'd like that?"

"Sure. I like having you around. It gives me a sense of security." I snickered. It crossed my mind that if I was amusing myself, I'd probably had a bit too much to drink.

Pete laughed. "I think you've had a little too much to drink." He stood up. "And I'd better go. I have a meeting at 8:00 tomorrow."

"Ugh. That's early."

"And you have to be at work at 8:00 tomorrow."

"8:30. That extra half hour makes all the difference."

"Right." He looked down at me, shaking his head but smiling. Right at that moment he looked like everything I wanted.

I stood up and held out my hand. "I think you should stay a little longer."

He was suddenly serious. "I think that might be a bad idea."

"Why?" Then it hit me. "You're seeing someone else."

He made a "you've got to be kidding" face. "No, I'm not. When would I have time to do that?"

"I don't know." Then something worse hit me. "Or you just don't want me."

He sighed and shook his head. "You know that's not it. If I thought you were serious, I'd be on you in a heartbeat. But you have had too much to drink, at least to be making that kind of decision. I think you'd regret it in the morning. And I don't want to do anything with you that you're going to regret."

"Oh, fuck that. Why don't you let me decide what I might or might not regret?" I moved closer to him and slid my hands under his t-shirt. "Come on. Stay."

Chapter 7
Monday, June 4

Pete left around 5:00 the next morning. During a break in the action, we'd had a discussion about just exactly what it was we thought we were doing by sleeping together. I'd voted for a best-friends-with-benefits relationship. Pete wanted more but was willing to try it my way for now. He didn't understand why I didn't want to date. I tried to explain that if we dated, then the potential was there to break up. If we weren't dating, we couldn't break up. It made sense to me at the time. Pete had just shaken his head, but he'd agreed.

I'd slept better than I had in weeks. When I woke up, the sun was rising and the birds were singing. I tried to decide whether I regretted last night. In the sense that I didn't want to lead Pete on, yes. But I'd explained myself to him, so I didn't think I was giving him any false hope.

But if Pete regretted it, then I regretted that.

But physically? I didn't regret it at all. After four years, I'd forgotten how good it was to be with him.

From the standpoint of my asthma, I was feeling better, although not yet back to normal. My peak flow was only 86%. The air quality in the city was still not great. I decided to leave for work early and go for a swim. The North Pool on campus opened for recreational swimming at 6:00 am. I was there by 6:30.

There were a limited number of people who regularly swam this early in the morning, and I knew them all. I waved hello to a couple of familiar faces as I walked onto the pool deck, then got into the water. I swam for 45 minutes, long enough for a good workout, then climbed out and retrieved my towel. As I did, I saw a face that I didn't recognize. An attractive woman, a few years older than me, shaking her hair out of her swim cap. She saw me looking at her and smiled. "Hi."

"Hi. Sorry if I was staring. It's just that I haven't seen you here before."

She laughed. "Yeah, this is early for me. I'm usually here on my lunch hour. But today I have a lunch meeting, so…" She tipped her head and regarded me, looking at me like… Was she *flirting* with me?

Time to go. I turned for the men's showers. "Cool. Nice to…um…" We hadn't met, so I couldn't say nice to meet you. "Hope you enjoyed it."

She raised her chin, flipped her hair back and her towel over her shoulder, and gave me a little smirk. "Oh, I did." She sauntered off.

Good grief.

In spite of two hot showers, I was still feeling a little short of breath. When I got to the office, I took a puff from my rescue inhaler. Usually the dusty library smell didn't bother me, but today it was. My airways were hypersensitive to everything right now.

I had forgotten until I opened the door to my office that I didn't have a computer. Damn. I needed to get my head back in the game. I hadn't heard back from Detective Blake yet. I moved my keyboard and mouse to the side, opened my laptop, and got to work.

The first thing I did was send an email to Dr. Oliver. I told him that I would like to take him up on his offer of more information about his research, and requested a tour of his lab. I also mentioned that I had a friend who was interested in donating to a foundation that funded stem cell research, and asked if I could bring said friend along.

He answered very quickly. Yes, he'd be happy to give me a tour of the lab, and yes, by all means, bring my friend. Would Wednesday morning at 9:00 work?

I sent Pete a quick text. *Stem cell lab Wed 9 am. Oliver says fine to bring you. OK?*

He answered quickly. *Fine. Will pick u up 8:30.*

I rolled my eyes at Pete's text-speak spelling, then turned back to the computer and answered Dr. Oliver. *9:00 is fine; we'll see you then. Thank you.*

Then I turned to my real work.

About an hour later, IT Andy was at my door.

"Hey, Dr. B. Sorry for the delay. I finally got free to work on your computer."

I'd forgotten to tell IT that I'd turned the computer over to the police. "Oh, hey. Actually, I turned my PC tower over to the UCLA police, the computer crimes guy, on Friday afternoon."

Andy looked shocked. "You did? Why?"

"Because some other weird things have been happening to me, and I thought the hacks to my computer might be related to that. If the cops can figure out who's been messing with my computer, they may be able to find out who's behind the other attacks."

Andy paled. "Attacks? What attacks?"

"My tires got slashed the other day, and someone tried to break into my apartment Saturday night."

"Wow." Andy looked worried. "Well, I guess that's cool, but I'm gonna have to tell my boss about it."

"Yeah, that's fine. The detective will probably contact him anyway."

"Okay… I'll have to bring you a new tower. It might take a couple of days. We don't have that many to go around with the budget cuts."

"That's fine. I can improvise until you can bring me a new one."

Andy agreed and left. The rest of the morning was uneventful, and I was getting ready to eat lunch when I saw an email from Karen Lewis.

Jamie - here is your Welsh language article. Have fun translating. -Karen

I opened the article. It was six pages long, and had several tables. I copied the article, opened Google Translate, and pasted the article into it. The translation popped up in the second window. I moved the translation into a Word document. It looked to be just as scrambled as the citation had been. Great. The unscrambling would take forever.

I saved the Word doc to Dropbox. Then, it occurred to me to change all my passwords to every app and site where I had an account, using the few Gaelic words I knew to make them as complicated as I could. Until I knew what was going on, I wanted to make it as difficult as possible for anyone who might be looking for anything about me or trying to mess with me. I also changed the password on my laptop. Just in case.

We were only moderately busy at reference. Clinton barely had to wait when he arrived at 1:30.

"Hi, Clinton."

"The word for the day is *velleity*." He bowed and walked away.

Liz looked the word up. "Willpower in its weakest form. That would be me with ice cream."

That would be me with Pete, I thought.

I was back in my office after my reference shift when Harley Buhrman showed up.

Harley was a throwback to the days of traveling encyclopedia salesmen. He was in his sixties, pear-shaped, with a dyed combover, a cheap suit, and scuffed loafers. He had an ingratiating manner and wore far too much cologne. Drakkar Noir cologne.

Oh, *shit*. I should have met him outside.

I jumped to my feet. Harley started to step into my office. "Dr. Brodie, good afternoon! I brought…"

I didn't hear the rest. Harley was drenched in Drakkar Noir, and it was attacking my airways. I grabbed my inhaler from my desk drawer and waved Harley back. "Get out! Get out! You can't…" I had to stop and try to take a breath. I took a puff from the inhaler, with no relief. That inhaler was empty now. I tossed it on my desk.

"Harley! Get out! NOW!" I shoved him out the door and ran down the stairs to the circulation desk. It was getting much harder to breathe, and my chest hurt. I grabbed the top of the circulation desk to steady myself. Liz had stopped there and was staring at me.

"Are you okay?"

"No!" I had to stop. I only had breath enough for one word at a time. "Asthma..." breathe... "call..." breathe...

But Liz was already dialing the campus emergency number. I leaned on the counter and concentrated on breathing. *Slow down, don't panic, slow down...* But it wasn't working.

Dr. Loomis appeared. "Jamie! What on earth..."

"He's having an asthma attack. I called the paramedics." Liz leaned in so I could see her face. "Is there any other medicine in your office? Is there anything else we can do?"

I pointed at Harley, who had overcome the shock of being shoved and was nearing the desk. "Keep..." breathe... "him..." breathe... "away..." breathe... "from me." Breathe. "Cologne."

"Oh my God." It occurred to me that I'd never heard Dr. Loomis say that. "Mr. Buhrman, please leave the premises."

Harley was sputtering. "But – but – I didn't know…"

"Dr. Brodie has a warning sign posted on his door. I can't imagine how you missed it." Dr. Loomis took Harley by the arm and nearly dragged him to the door. "Get out of the building and stay out. Do not come back today. Do not come back at all unless you clear it through me personally. Liz, please retrieve Mr. Buhrman's briefcase."

Harley was still sputtering. "Now, wait just a minute…"

Dr. Loomis lost her cool a little. If I'd been well enough, this scene would have been entertaining. "Mr. Buhrman, I will have no more of this. Are you going to leave now, or should I have campus police remove you?" She opened the door for Harley, who stumbled out of it. "I want to see you heading for the parking structure. NOW."

She closed that door, and opened another for the paramedics. I was gasping for breath, but the attack seemed to have slowed in its progression. I wasn't going to pass out this time. The paramedics got me hooked to oxygen and the monitors and strapped me onto the stretcher.

Dr. Loomis was in full charge mode. "Liz, please, take Jamie's computer bag from his office and accompany him to the emergency room. Please report back as soon as possible." She turned to me and patted me on the arm. Somewhere, in the still-oxygenated part of my brain, I was shocked again. "Do what the doctors tell you. Take as much time as you need. I don't want to see you back here until you are well."

I nodded weakly. "Yes..." breathe... "ma'am." She nodded, and turned to the paramedics. "Off you go, gentlemen."

Off we went. It only took a few minutes to get to the UCLA Medical Center ER. The paramedics rolled me back to a cubicle, and the nurse clipped a pulse oximeter to my finger. I scooted my butt over to the ER bed, and a nurse and one of the paramedics helped me get my shirt off over the IVs the paramedics had started.

A very young guy in a short white coat that was way too clean stepped around the curtain. "Mr. Brodie? Dr. Waverly. How are you feeling?"

Oh, hell, no. I glared, and pointed at him. "Intern."

"Uh, yeah." The intern looked nonplussed. "So - what happened?"

The nurse brought the bed's head up to a nearly 90 degree position and propped pillows behind me, then patted them. I leaned back, and she slipped a mask over my face. Oxygen, and something moist. No medication in it yet. I glared at the intern again. "Cologne." Breathe. "Asthma." Breathe. "Boom."

"Okay." Dr. Intern was writing. "So you had previously been diagnosed with asthma?"

I made an exasperated sound and looked at the nurse beseechingly. She laughed. "Dr. Waverly, why don't you see if Dr. Suzuki is available?"

"Right." Waverly gave me a dirty look and left. I snorted. The nurse chuckled. "Yeah, he thinks he's all that. He'll learn."

"Not..." breathe... "on me."

The nurse grinned. "Nope, not on you. Here comes the real doctor."

I'd seen Dr. Suzuki before and was glad to see him now. Suzuki walked in, carrying my chart.

"Jamie! What happened to you?"

"Cologne." Breathe. "A lot of it."

"Does this feel like a typical attack for you?"

I nodded. Suzuki turned to the nurse. "Can we get an albuterol nebulizer set up, please?"

"On it." The nurse headed out.

"Had you been feeling short of breath before today?"

I nodded. "Thursday. Funeral. Outdoors. Flowers. Smog. More. Inhaler. Since. Then." The effort of talking was wearing me out.

"Okay." The nurse arrived with the nebulizer. "Let's get this on you."

As soon as the medication started flowing, I felt my chest easing. Sweet relief. "Better..." breathe... "already."

"Good." Suzuki smiled. "You just hang out and breathe. We'll check your oxygenation again in about 15 minutes."

"Thanks."

Suzuki left; the nurse was cleaning up my arm around the hastily-inserted IV. "Do you need us to call someone?"

"Brother. Number in phone."

She handed me my phone. I found Kevin's number and called then handed the phone to her. She listened, and mouthed "voicemail" at me. "Mr. Brodie, this is Carol Braithwaite at UCLA Med Center ER. Your brother is here as a patient and he asked that we call you first. I'll call his next contact." She hung up and turned back to me. "Who's your next contact?"

Damn. I was going to have to call Pete. I found his number in my phone and handed it to the nurse. She dialed; I heard him answer. "Hey." He thought it was me.

"Um, hi, Mr. Ferguson, this is Carol Braithwaite at UCLA Med Center ER…" She paused. I could hear Pete's voice, but not his words.

"Yes, he's going to be fine, but he's had an asthma attack. He'll have to be here a bit longer, but he'll need a ride home eventually. I tried his brother's cell but he doesn't answer." Another pause.

"Will do. Thank you." Carol hung up. "He said he'll be right here. Where's he coming from?"

"Santa Monica."

"Okay, then it shouldn't take too long. How are you feeling now?"

"Better."

"Great. I'm going to go get a couple of things, and I'll be right back. You just relax."

Easier said than done, but I was feeling better. Liz came in for a few minutes to drop off my computer bag. She was still there when Dr. Suzuki came in again and listened to my lungs, then ordered another dose of the nebulizer. He turned to Liz for a minute. "Do you happen to know what brand of cologne caused Jamie's attack?"

Liz made a face. "It was Drakkar Noir. My uncle used to wear it. I always hated it."

Suzuki nodded and made a note in my chart. The nurse arrived with the nebulizer, and Liz said goodbye.

I was resting, nebulizer mask on my face, when Pete arrived, looking frantic. "What happened?"

I made a face. "Sales rep. Nasty cologne."

"Oh, for God's sake. Did he not see the sign on your door?"

"He's an. Idiot." I scrunched up my face at Pete. "Sorry."

"Not your fault. You'd have been fine if not for the salesman, right?"

I nodded.

"They won't keep you overnight, will they?"

"Doubt it."

"I've got a 6:45 class. I'll call and get Jane to put a note on the door. Tell them to log into the course website instead. I'll post something on there for them to do." He looked me over. "Your color is not too bad."

I nodded. "Feeling better."

"Thank God." Pete sighed in relief. "Where's Kev?"

"Didn't answer. Busy."

"That shit happens." He looked at me gravely. "I'm glad you called me."

I shrugged. "You're on. Short list."

He laughed. "Good."

I had to stay in the ER for nearly five more hours. My own doctor, Dr. Weikal, stopped in at some point to see me. He read over my chart, listened to my lungs, and left instructions to make an appointment to see him within 48 hours.

My phone rang twice. Once it was Kevin; Pete talked to him. The second time was a number I didn't recognize, so we didn't answer it, and it went to voice mail. Dr. Suzuki wouldn't discharge me until my peak flow was back up to 80%, and it took a while. Finally, by 9:00, we were making the short drive to my apartment in Pete's Jeep with a couple of new prescriptions and an appointment with my primary care doctor for Wednesday.

When we pulled into the parking lot, we saw the fire trucks.

"Oh, shit." I just knew it was our apartment.

Pete tried to be logical. "It's not necessarily your place."

But it was.

A firefighter stopped us as we walked toward the building. I showed him my driver's license to prove that I lived there, and he allowed us through. I walked into the door of the apartment and stopped so fast that Pete ran into me.

The place was completely trashed. Every cabinet door in the kitchen was open, and everything had been pulled out, opened and dumped or broken. Flour, cereal, and fragments of plates and glasses coated the counters and floor. The refrigerator was open, and everything in it had been emptied. Every piece of furniture had been overturned, and those with any padding had been slit open. The TV and stereo were smashed. Kevin stood in the middle of the room, his face white with fury. His partner, Tim Garcia, was talking to him and a firefighter, and a couple of crime scene techs were dusting for fingerprints and sifting through the mess.

But that was nothing compared to the scene in my bedroom.

All of my books, clothes and shoes, and the towels from the bathroom, had been piled on top of my bed and set on fire. The fire was out, but the smell was atrocious, a mix of burning rubber and something else equally noxious. Everything was destroyed, down to the box spring under my mattress. I was in such deep shock that I didn't even notice that I was short of breath until Pete leaned in behind me and said, "Hey, we've got to get you out of here. You can't be breathing in this crap."

I turned and looked at him. The look on my face must have frightened him. He took my arm and guided me back into the living room. The firefighter spotted us and walked over. "Lt. Evers. I'm an arson investigator. You're Detective Brodie's brother?"

"Yes, sir. This is Pete Ferguson."

Evers shook Pete's hand. Pete asked, "What happened?"

Evers turned back and looked at the room. "They came in through the sliding glass door in the bedroom. So far we haven't found much in terms of evidence. We know accelerant was used, but we're not sure what yet, except that it wasn't gasoline." He turned back to me. "It's hard to see if anything is missing because of the mess. Kevin hasn't noticed anything yet. We'll need you both to take a closer look at some point."

"Sure."

"We'll need to take your fingerprints too, so we can exclude yours from the ones the techs are lifting."

"Sure." That seemed to be all I was capable of saying. I reached for the inhaler in my jacket. The smoke was definitely getting to me now.

Pete asked Evers, "Can we go outside for this? We came here from the emergency room. Jamie had a bad asthma attack this morning, and he spent most of the day there. He needs to get out of this smoke."

"Absolutely." Evers went back to where Tim and Kevin were standing. "Tim, the brother's here, but he's getting over an asthma attack and needs to get out of the smoke."

Kevin hadn't noticed I was there. He whirled around at me. "What are you doing in here?" He grabbed my arm and started hauling me outside.

"Stop dragging me." I yanked my arm out of his grip and kept walking. We made it to the outside stairs, and I turned to face all of them.

Kevin paled at the look on my face, and Tim started moving towards the bench at the end of the hall. "Why don't we sit? I need to ask you some questions."

"Sure." Again. I sat on the bench, and sagged. I was exhausted.

Tim pulled out a notebook. "Do you have any idea who might have done this?"

I shook my head. "Not who, no. But I might know why." I gave him the basics, with Kevin and Pete filling in when I got too short of breath - Dan's death, his letter, the articles, the visit from Oliver, meeting Goldstein at the funeral, the computer attack, and the attempted break-in at the apartment. "All I've been doing is research into these two articles, and I haven't even turned up anything suspicious in my research. But someone seems to be trying to discourage me from looking."

Tim looked unhappy. "Where was this death?"

"Cedars-Sinai."

"That's Wilshire Division. I'll talk to whoever took the call and see what the status is on the autopsy."

"Don't bother." Kevin was leaning against the opposite wall, scowling, his arms folded. "I already did. No sign of foul play."

"Okay, but I'll call and get a copy of it for this file." Tim turned back to me. "The fire was on your bed. It wouldn't be a stretch to think that this was focused on you."

"No." I sighed. "And whoever is behind this either doesn't know about Kevin, or doesn't care, right? Anyone that would willfully incur the wrath of the LAPD must be nuts, right?"

Tim snorted. "That'd be one way to describe it." He tucked his notebook into his pocket. "Let's get you fingerprinted. Then you can get out of here. There's nothing else you can do in there tonight. Tomorrow, after the place has aired out and the crowds are gone, you can go through and see if anything's missing and if anything's salvageable. You gonna bunk with Ferguson tonight?"

What? "Uh - no -"

"Yes, he is." Pete's tone said he would brook no argument.

Kevin chimed in. "Good."

I whirled on him. "Where are you going?"

"To Abby's sister's. She's already there. And no, you can't come."

Pete slapped me on the back. It looked hearty, for public consumption, but was gentle. "C'mon. You're dead on your feet. There's plenty of space for you in the guest room."

I got fingerprinted, and we were released. We headed to the parking lot. I turned in the direction of my assigned slot, then remembered that my VW was still in the shop, getting its tires replaced. I groaned. Pete heard me.

"No worries. We'll get your car tomorrow. You're in no shape to drive tonight anyway."

I wanted to argue with him but couldn't dredge up the energy. We were silent on the way to Pete's townhouse. As soon as we were in the door, the full force of the day hit me, and my knees nearly buckled. Pete grabbed my arms and guided me to the sofa. "Take your shoes off. I need to change the sheets on my bed."

"No." I waved at him weakly. "Don't do that. Put me in the guest room."

"There aren't any sheets on that bed at all, so it doesn't matter. Besides, if I'm with you, I'll notice if you start having trouble with your breathing again. I'm gonna get you a bathrobe, and you can get undressed."

He disappeared up the stairs. I started pulling off my shoes and socks. I was anxious to get out of my clothes, and I needed a shower. My body was completely drained, but my brain was wired from the side effects of all the meds I'd had over the course of the day. I felt grungy from the hospital, and I smelled like smoke.

Pete reappeared with a bathrobe. "Here. You can use the guest bathroom and leave your clothes in there. I'll toss them in the washer. Do you want pajamas?"

"Do you have a pair of gym shorts?"

"Coming right up." He headed back up the stairs. I left my computer bag on the sofa and followed him, then turned off into the guest bathroom. I dropped my clothes on the toilet lid and put on the robe, then headed for the master bedroom.

Pete was putting the comforter back on the bed. "I put a pair of shorts in there." He indicated the master bath with his head. "There are clean towels in there and a new toothbrush. Help yourself to shampoo or whatever else you need."

I nodded. I was too tired to form words. The shower had a seat molded into its shape; I turned on the water and sat down. Once I was done and dry, I put on the shorts and the robe, brushed my teeth, and headed for the kitchen.

Pete was starting the washing machine. "Feel better?"

"Cleaner, anyway."

"Well, that's a start. Want something to eat?"

I didn't feel hungry, but I hadn't eaten since breakfast. "I guess I'd better. But not much."

"How about tomato soup? Some crackers?"

"Actually, that sounds great." I sat down at the little dining table.

After we ate I needed to check my peak flow again, but realized the flow meter had been in the apartment. I wasn't going to do anything about that tonight; I'd get it replaced in the morning. I rubbed my face. I was whipped, but the worst side effect of all the drugs dumped into me over the course of the day was a jittery exhaustion that made sleep impossible. So there wasn't any point in going to bed. Pete arranged a mass of pillows on the sofa, and I propped myself up with my laptop and a glass of water. Pete went out briefly to get my prescriptions filled, then settled on the love seat to grade papers.

I leaned back and closed my eyes, but sleep wouldn't come. I decided to take a crack at rearranging the translated Welsh article. I wasn't going to be able to read anything tonight, but maybe I could unscramble some of it.

I pulled the document out of Dropbox and paged through it. The article was arranged in sections, similar to the research articles I was used to seeing – abstract, introduction, review of literature, hypothesis, methodology, statistical analysis, results, discussion. I decided to start with the methodology. That would be the most interesting comparison to Oliver, Wray, and Goldsmith's article. I took a deep breath – at least as deep as I was able to – and jumped in.

About an hour later, Pete looked up. "What are you doing?"

"I didn't get a chance to tell you. The Welsh-language article came today. I'd run it through the translator and saved it before Harley came in."

"You're working on that *now?*"

"Well, I have to do something. I'm still juiced from the drugs. The worst of it will wear off in a couple of hours…" breathe "…and I'll be able to sleep, but until then I might as well accomplish something. And I can't do anything that requires concentration or precision."

Pete just shook his head. I turned back to the article. I'd almost finished with the methodology section. The terminology sounded very similar to that of the Americans' article, but that was no surprise. If the successful procedure was a modification of the earlier one, the methodologies should be similar.

I completed the last paragraph of the section, saved it, and logged off. It was after midnight now. The jitters were wearing off and exhaustion was stealing over me. I checked email before shutting down. Nothing important, except for a message from Detective Blake.

Dr. Brodie,

We've taken a preliminary look at your computer and haven't found any evidence that it was hacked into from outside the UCLA network. I interviewed Ms. DeLong today, and she denied having done anything to your computer. She was quite upset by my questions, however.

We have several other things to look at, and I will let you know the outcome. Just wanted to let you know that, so far, this looks like an inside job.

Regards,
Roger Blake

The possibility of an inside job was the only logical explanation. But who at UCLA would want to do that? I didn't remember any students getting mad at me. And it was hard to imagine Roberta, the unfriendly staff assistant, going to these lengths.

I yawned. Pete looked up, then laid down his book and stood up. "Okay. Time for bed."

I didn't argue.

I'd been in Pete's bed before, but not this one. He'd upgraded since we'd dated. I slipped in between the clean, soft sheets and almost groaned with pleasure. I wouldn't mind sleeping here for a few nights.

That thought snapped me back to wakefulness. I couldn't stay here for long. This would be pushing friends with benefits too far, way too much like a real relationship. It wouldn't be fair to Pete.

And it scared me. Because, if I was really, truly honest with myself, I was already a little bit in love with Pete.

Maybe even more than a little bit.

So I couldn't stay here long.

But where could I go?

I'd have to talk to our apartment manager. Maybe there was a studio apartment I could sublet or get a short-term lease on while our place was being repaired.

Finding a place of my own was probably a good idea anyway. When Kevin and I had first moved in together, we were fresh off our divorces (that's what Ethan's breakup had felt like to me). Neither one of us wanted to be alone. Now Abby was there. She and Kevin didn't have any plans to get married, but even so I was starting to feel like the third wheel, in spite of the fact that my name was still on the lease. But neither one of them would ever ask me to move. At least I didn't think they would. So I'd have to do it on my own.

No time like the present.

I could kill two birds with one stone. Find a place of my own to get out of Pete's house and to give Kevin and Abby more privacy. And I liked our apartment complex a lot; I could get a studio apartment there and still be close by Kevin and Abby in case they needed help with anything.

Okay. I'd try to do that tomorrow.

Chapter 8

Tuesday, June 5

I slept late the next day. When I woke up, Pete was gone and the sun was streaming in the cracks between the blinds. I rolled over and looked at the clock. It was 9:30. Shit. I'd slept longer than I'd intended. My bladder was screaming at me to get up.

I swung my feet over the edge of the bed, sat up, and was overcome with a wave of dizziness. God, I felt terrible. I sat there to clear my head and took stock. My head hurt a little. My rib cage hurt a lot. Every breath was a reminder of the strain my rib muscles had been under yesterday. I had random bruises on my arms, a couple from IV insertions, and a couple that I couldn't identify. Probably got banged on the stretcher or something.

And I had no clothes.

The dizziness passed, and I stood up. I went into the bathroom to find my clothes from yesterday folded and stacked on the toilet lid. I sniffed them; the smoky smell was gone. Pete had washed, dried, and folded them. I sighed. I could get used to being treated this well, and that was a problem.

I took a longish shower, letting the hot water beat on my ribs and the steam penetrate my lungs. I washed my hair again; I might be imagining it, but it still smelled smoky to me.

I dried off, and realized I had no toiletries. Crap. I looked around and didn't see anything. I walked back into the bedroom and saw that I had missed another thoughtful gesture from Pete. On top of the dresser was a new deodorant, razor, and a tube of travel toothpaste. He'd left a note as well: "I had these already, help yourself."

I could *really* get used to this.

I had to get out of here.

I was eating breakfast when Pete got home. I'd put my clothes from yesterday back on, but I felt overdressed. He came in and dropped his computer bag at the door. He looked tired.

"Hey. You found your clothes."

"Yeah. Thanks for doing that for me."

"No problem." He got a bottle of Coke out of the fridge and leaned on the counter. "I figured that was easiest. And they smelled like smoke."

I washed my bowl and spoon and remembered that I hadn't looked at my phone since yesterday in the emergency room. There was one voice mail. I started listening - oh, shit. It was from Diane. I must have turned paler than usual because Pete said, "What's wrong?"

I put the phone on speaker and started the message over.

"Hello, Jamie Brodie, you fucking ASSHOLE! Guess what? I just had a visit from the fucking UCLA cops asking me if I had sabotaged your fucking computer. The answer to that is FUCK NO! How could you *think* that? You *asshole!!* Here's another question: are you and I still friends? The answer to that is FUCK NO! Fuck you! And the horse you rode in on! You can go fuck yourself! Or better yet, get one of your PIG friends to do it! But no, wait, you'd like that too much! So just fuck off! I never want to see your fucking face again! GOODBYE!"

There was silence for a moment. I erased the message. Pete made like Mr. Spock. "Fascinating."

I groaned. "I was going to call her yesterday morning, then I got busy, then I had the attack."

"That was pretty nasty. And she doesn't have much of a vocabulary."

I put my head in my hands. "I don't know if I can fix that."

Pete sat down across from me. "I'm not sure you should try. At least not today."

And my phone rang.

I looked at the caller ID; it was a UCLA number. "Hello?"

"Jamie." It was Liz. "How are you feeling?"

"Hey. Better, definitely."

"Oh, that's great. I was afraid they were going to keep you overnight."

"Nah. I've got to be a lot closer to death for them to do that."

"Oh, don't even joke about that. Listen, I wanted to tell you something. That girl that was in your class in library school? The one with the orange Mohawk?"

Uh oh. "Diane DeLong."

"Yeah, her. She was here late yesterday looking for you. She was really mad and made a scene. Dr. Loomis had to ask her to leave."

"Oh, shit. I'm sorry about that. Will you apologize to Dr. Loomis for me?"

"Sure. But she doesn't blame you." Liz paused. "You know, I never wanted to tell you this because she was your friend, but Diane used to make some really homophobic remarks when you weren't around. Not against you personally, but in general. And also sometimes about Mark Gladwell, who was in my class. Remember him?"

I did. Mark had been young, small, and effeminate. And not yet out. He would have been an easy target. "Well, she said some pretty homophobic things in her message. And she used the P word in reference to my cop friends. And I don't mean P for police."

"Wow. Maybe she's not such a loss."

"Maybe. But I've got bigger problems than her right now." I told Liz about the fire.

"Oh my God! Do we need to start an emergency drive for you?"

I laughed. A little. "No, I'm fine. Relatively speaking. I'm staying at Pete's for now." That got a look from Pete. "And my computer bag was with me, and I have the clothes I was wearing. And I think I had laundry in my car, which is still at the shop. And we had renter's insurance, so I'll get a check at some point. So don't start collecting anything."

"When are you coming back to work?"

"Tomorrow." That got another look from Pete.

"Okay. I'll tell Dr. Loomis."

We hung up.

Pete's voice was soft. "What do you mean you're staying here *for now*?"

I cleared my throat. "Well, I was thinking. Who knows how long it's going to take for them to get our place fixed? Kevin's fine at Abby's sister's, but I can't impose on you for an indefinite time. I can check with our apartment manager and see if they have any studio apartments that are going to be empty just for the summer. That way I'd be back near campus and out of your hair."

Pete's face was a mask. "Why would you think that I want you out of my hair? You're not imposing on me."

"Yeah, but -"

He smacked his hand on the table and stood up. "Damn it, Jamie!" He turned away from me, then walked upstairs.

I lowered my head and slowly, gently banged it on the table. Then I went upstairs. "Pete?"

He was in the guest room, at his computer. He didn't turn to face me. "What?"

"I'm gonna take the bus to Westwood. I have to pick up the VW."

That made him turn around. Then he stood up and picked up his keys from the desk. "You're not taking the bus. Don't be an idiot."

I didn't say anything. I followed him out the door and to his Jeep. We drove in silence to the garage. He waited until I was sure that the VW was ready to go, then gave me the door key to the condo. "In case I'm not there when you get back."

I just nodded.

I didn't hear what I wanted to from the apartment manager. "The studios are really popular right now. We don't have one available, unless someone breaks a lease, and I don't expect that to happen." She smiled sympathetically. "I'm glad you enjoy living here so much. I'm going to put the pressure on to get your place restored as quickly as possible. We should have you back in there in less than a month."

I thanked her. I was going to have to gut it out at Pete's.

Since I had my car, I went to Target in Culver City. In spite of what I'd told Liz, I really didn't have anything to my name except a computer and a car and the clothes on my back. Target opened up to me like an old friend. I bought socks, underwear, swim trunks, gym shorts, lots of t-shirts, a couple of pairs of pajama pants, sweatpants and hoodies, a couple of pairs of jeans, a bunch of polo shirts, and a couple of pairs of chinos. I wasn't going to get dress shirts here; I could get away with wearing polo shirts to work. I did have a pair of running shoes in the back of the VW, and I had the shoes I'd been wearing yesterday, so I could get by there as well until I could get to Penney's or someplace with a better shoe selection. I bought toothbrushes, toothpaste, shampoo, razors, deodorant, soap, and towels. I went to the pharmacy and replaced my flowmeter. And I bought beer and Coke Classic and a huge box of Cheez-Its. Comfort food.

I was getting in the VW when Kevin called. He had just met with the insurance adjuster, who had cut him a check on the spot. He was depositing it into our joint account, so when the funds became available in a few days I could transfer half to my account.

Then he asked, "Where are you?"

I told him and filled him in on the other events of the morning.

Then he proceeded to yell at me.

He yelled at me for picking up the car, for going to the apartment complex, for going shopping. He yelled at me for the way I was treating Pete. He yelled at me for thinking that I wouldn't continue to be welcome in my own home with him and Abby. He yelled at me for even thinking of going back to work tomorrow, and he yelled at me for having been friends with "that pink-haired loon" - Diane - in the first place.

He ended with, "What the hell is the matter with you?"

I said, "I don't know." And hung up on him.

Then I sat in the parking lot and called my dad.

My dad and I were always close. He was close to all of us; he'd raised us, with help from our grandfather, after our mom was killed by a drunk driver when I was six months old. But after Jeff and Kevin had gone off to college and my granddad moved back to South Carolina, it was just me and my dad for a year. I'd always been able to talk to him about anything. And I really needed to talk to him now.

When he answered the phone, "Hey, sport, what's up?" I had to struggle to fight back the tears.

The first thing I managed to get out was, "I just hung up on Kevin."

"Okay, why'd you do that?"

"Because he was yelling at me."

"Okay, why was he yelling at you?"

And that's how it went. Eventually I calmed down enough to stop sniffling and spill my guts.

My dad was quiet through the whole story. When I got to the asthma attack and the fire, he was aghast. "Jamie! If someone is after you up there, then the last thing you need is to be by yourself. Why do you not want to stay with Pete?"

I tried to explain it to him. He wasn't buying it. "Son, you don't give Pete enough credit. He obviously cares about you, and he's a much higher quality person than those last three or four guys were. And he's *definitely* not Ethan. You need to change trains here. Get off the Ethan train before the Pete train leaves the station and it's too late."

"I *am* off the Ethan train."

"No, you're not. You're still letting him color every relationship you have, seven years later. He'd be amazed to learn that he has this power over you. You didn't let him rule your life while you were with him, so why are you letting him rule it now?"

A flash of insight that I didn't know I had until I opened my mouth. "Because it's safer this way."

"Well, apparently not, since you tell me your life is a disaster." Dad paused. I could almost hear him deciding what to say. "Listen. I wouldn't worry about Diane. She's the one who needs to apologize to you. Kevin will forgive you, and he shouldn't be yelling at you anyway. But Pete is not going to put his life on hold forever waiting for you to come to your senses. And it's time for you to do that. To come to your senses, I mean. If the universe is pushing you in one direction, which it clearly is, then trying to maintain your position is pointless. It expends a lot of energy, and you won't win. Tell me the truth. Do you have feelings for Pete?"

"Well, yeah – I mean, um…" I stopped. And admitted it. "Yeah, I do."

"Then for Pete's sake, pun intended, get back to his place and tell him."

I groaned. "It's not that easy."

"Yes, it is. At least talk to him. Graciously accept his offer of staying with him, apologize to him for being an idiot, and see where it goes."

I sighed. "I'll try."

"Okay. And tell Kevin that I said to stop yelling at you."

I laughed a little. "I will definitely do that."

We hung up. I sat there for a few more minutes, staring off into the distance. Then I started the car.

By the time I got back to the condo, it was nearly 7:00. Pete was home when I got there. I'd been half afraid he wouldn't be and half afraid he would. I dropped my stuff at the foot of the stairs and collapsed onto one of the chairs at the dinette table, rubbing my face with my hands. Pete sat down across the table from me.

"What did the apartment manager say?"

"They don't have anything. They won't have anything for months unless someone breaks their lease. So, if your offer still stands to let me stay with you until our place is finished, then I accept."

"Of course it still stands. You're welcome to be here as long as you like." Then: "Jamie?"

"Yeah?"

"Why are you so resistant to letting me help you?"

I looked up at him. "It's not that I'm resistant..."

"Then what is it?" Pete was obviously in distress. I hated this. "What are you afraid of?"

I was too tired and stressed out for anything but honesty. "That you'll get the wrong idea."

"About what?"

"About me. About what I'm looking for from you. I'm not looking for anything from anyone. I can handle this myself. I can handle my life myself. I'm tired of being only seen as the little brother. I'm a grown man, and I can take care of myself."

Pete's face shifted to something gentler. "I don't see you as a little brother. I definitely see you as a grown man. I always have."

"Really?"

"Yes, really." Pete sighed. "I know you can take care of yourself, but why should you have to? None of us should have to. We're not made to go through life alone."

"I think maybe I was."

"No, you weren't. Listen to me. What Ethan did to you was inexcusable, but -"

"I do *not* want to talk about Ethan."

"Okay, let's talk about you. You were the one who said historians dwell on the past, and that's *exactly* what you're doing. Because of what Ethan did to you, you've shut yourself off from letting anyone else get close to you. From letting anyone else try to love you. You keep hooking up with these flimsy guys -"

"Flimsy guys? Is that a psychological term?"

"It should be. Flimsy guys. Guys without substance. You pick guys that you think won't stay with you so you can keep proving to yourself over and over that you're not worth staying with..."

I was getting mad. "Enough with the psychoanalysis, please?"

Pete was getting mad too. "I am not analyzing you. I am trying to convince you that you are your own worst enemy. I've watched you set yourself up for failure over and over and sink lower and lower in your own estimation, and it's killing me. It's *killing* me. Because..." His voice broke and he stopped.

I was almost afraid to ask. "Because why?"

His voice was softer. "Because it doesn't have to be that way. Because you're such a great guy, and you're definitely worth staying with. You're worth so much more than that. You deserve a guy who sees that and wants to build a life with you." He pushed back and stood up. "I'm not saying this very well."

"It's been a long day. Maybe you're not thinking very clearly."

He leaned back against the counter and put his hands in his pockets. "No, I'm thinking fine. But I'm afraid to tell you exactly what I feel, I guess."

That was supposed to be my line. "Why? You've just told me some pretty hard stuff."

He looked at his feet. "Because I'm afraid that I'll scare you away for good, because you're skittish, like a deer in a clearing. Because I don't want to lose what relationship we do have, because friends with benefits is better than nothing. Because..." He stopped, and looked up, right into my eyes. "Because I love you. I always have, since I first got to know you. And I'm afraid that you won't ever reciprocate that because you're so stuck in your past and so determined to prove that you're self-sufficient. You're convinced that every guy you get involved with is going to leave you, so you never trust anyone, and they do leave you. It's a downward spiral, like this vortex you're stuck in. And I'm reaching out to you, to drag you into the boat, and you won't take my hand. It breaks my heart."

I felt paralyzed. "Pete... Don't you see? If we did get together, and it didn't work out, it would be so much worse than any of those other guys. And you'd be hurt, and it would be my fault, and I couldn't stand that."

Pete shook his head and looked back at his feet. He said very quietly, "That's rationalization, and you know it." His face twisted, and he bit his lip to regain control. It didn't work. He turned away from me, put his hands on the counter, and leaned into them. He laughed, but his shoulders were sagging. "It's ironic, I guess. I've been wishing and hoping that we could get back together one day, and now you're here, but you don't want to stay."

Fuck. "Pete, it's not -"

He snapped his left hand up at me, elbow straight, traffic-cop style. *Stop, in the name of love*. "No."

I didn't move. I couldn't. Pete dropped his hand, straightened up, and walked past me to the stairs without looking at me. "Shower time." He started climbing.

I sat still. It was quiet here. Peaceful. I could hear muted bird chatter and a few rumbles of traffic from Wilshire. Pete's footsteps were muffled above me. Then I heard the faint hiss of the shower.

Shit, shit, shit.

The shower cut off, but Pete didn't come back down. I cut all the tags off of my new clothes and washed two loads, dried and folded all of it, then put everything back in the Target bags and carried them upstairs. I opened my new flow meter and checked my peak flow; it was at 82% of baseline. Not much better, but over the crucial 80% line. I readied my clothes for the following day, gathered up my laptop, and went to the living room.

I sat on the sofa with my laptop, Cheez-Its, and Coke close at hand and checked my email. Mostly routine stuff, but there was one that froze me in place. It was from the director of medical records at the hospital.

Dear Dr. Brodie,

At 3:30 am today, our automated system recorded an unauthorized access of your medical records. Unfortunately, some of your medical information may have been temporarily exposed before the system closed the breach.

We are working to determine the source of the access. In the meantime, we wanted you to be aware of this. We apologize for the problem. We have been able to determine that the access came from within the UCLA network.

If you have any questions, please do not hesitate to contact me.

Sincerely,

Gloria Silveira, Director of Medical Records, Ronald Reagan UCLA Medical Center

Shit. I emailed her back and cc'ed Detective Blake.

Ms. Silveira, thank you for informing me of this. I have been having problems with my office PC, and the computer crimes detective at the UCLA police is already investigating. I'm copying him on this so he can contact you to coordinate your investigations, which I feel must be related.

If you need any more information from me, please let me know.

I sat back. It was official.

My life was going to hell in a greased handbasket.

Chapter 9
Wednesday, June 6

The next morning, Pete and I tiptoed around each other politely. We didn't talk about anything from last night. We did finalize an approach to our visit with Dr. Oliver; Pete would claim to be looking for a fertility lab to fund. I told him he'd better dress rich.

"I don't have anything rich."

"Just wear your best suit. Or you could go with the tweedy academic look…"

He went with tweedy academic.

Fertility Research was on the third floor of a medical office building a block from Cedars. We parked close to the building this time. Pete turned off the engine and looked at me before we got out of the car. "You still think this is a good idea."

"Yeah, I do. We won't be here long or ask any questions that will give anything away. It will give me a glimpse into the atmosphere here; maybe we can tell if something seems off. And remember, you're supposed to be interested in investing, so you should do most of the talking."

"Yes. I've got it." He shook his head and opened his door. "Let's get this over with."

We rode the elevator up, following Dr. Oliver's directions, and turned right. Fertility Research had the southwest quadrant of the building. The first door on the left was the receptionist's office. I knocked and stuck my head in. "Hi. Dr. Brodie and Dr. Ferguson, here to see Dr. Oliver?"

"Hello, Dr. Brodie. Come right in." The receptionist was a grandmotherly looking lady in a blouse and a jumper with a cat embroidered on it. Her name plate said Marjorie Ellison. She gave us a sunny smile. "Would you like some coffee? Tea?"

We declined. Marjorie said, "Let me know if you change your minds." She lifted her phone and pushed a button. "Dr. Oliver, your visitors are here." She waited a minute, then said, "Yes, sir," and hung up. "He'll be right with you."

Pete was looking at some brochures that were on a side table. "May I have one of these?"

"Oh, yes, help yourself."

Pete picked up a couple of brochures and started reading. I smiled at Marjorie. She smiled back. It was very smiley in here.

Dr. Oliver appeared in just a couple of minutes. "Dr. Brodie! So good to see you again!" He shook my hand vigorously. I introduced Pete, and they shook hands also. Dr. Oliver regarded Pete with interest bordering on avarice. "Dr. Ferguson, it's a pleasure. I understand from Dr. Brodie that you're looking for a worthy cause in which to invest."

"Yes. I've come into some money that I need to give to charity for tax purposes. I'm sure you understand." Pete was playing the part of rich guy flawlessly. "I have a personal interest in fertility research, and I'm looking at different organizations, for a place that I feel comfortable donating to."

"Of course. I understand completely. We'd love to be the beneficiary of your generosity. Allow me to make a good impression on you." Oliver chuckled; Pete chuckled with him. Wow, he was really good at this.

"Come with me, and let me show you our lab. It's our pride and joy." We said goodbye to Marjorie and headed down the hallway.

The lab took up the entire right side of the hallway. There was a door at the front of the room and one at the back. We walked in to a brightly lit, mostly white space. It was about what I expected: several rows of lab benches with whirring, blinking machines and a few people standing at them in white coats.

One of the people looked up at our entry and walked toward us. Smiling, of course. Then she saw me, and her jaw dropped in recognition at exactly the same moment as mine. It was the flirting woman from the pool. She was wearing jeans and a turtleneck under her long, white lab coat. Her streaked blonde hair was pulled back in a ponytail. She recovered first. "*Oh.* You're the early morning swimmer."

I wasn't recovering from my shock very quickly. "Yeah…um…" I held my hand out. "Jamie Brodie."

She took my hand and held it warmly. "Alana Wray. Isn't this a coincidence!" She seemed delighted.

No. Fucking. *Way*.

Dr. Oliver looked intrigued; Pete looked confused. Oliver asked, "Have you met before?"

Dr. Wray let go of my hand and put her hands on her hips, tilting her head the same way she had the other day. *Still flirting?* "We have, very briefly, at the UCLA pool Monday morning. Remember, Tristan, we had that lunch meeting with the board, and I had to swim in the morning? This lovely young man welcomed me to the morning swim."

Oliver rubbed his hands together. "Well! How serendipitous!"

Not exactly the word I would have used. But I wasn't sure what word I *would* use. Where was Clinton when you needed him?

Pete and Dr. Wray introduced themselves and shook hands. Wray beamed at both of us. "Welcome, both of you! We don't get many visitors."

"Thank you for letting us interrupt your day." Pete had recovered, but his expression was guarded.

"Oh, you're not interrupting." She turned to Oliver. "Tristan, would you like me to show them around?"

I was watching Oliver, mostly so I didn't have to look at Wray or Pete. Oliver seemed a bit uncomfortable with the idea of Wray giving us the tour. "No, thank you, I'll take care of it." It was subtle, but his attitude hinted at being patronizing. Hmm.

It didn't seem to bother Dr. Wray much. She shrugged and smiled at me, as if to say, *What are you gonna do*? "Let me know if you have any questions." She went back to the station she'd left when we came in.

Oliver walked us toward the back of the room. "Here's where the process starts." He pointed out a couple of machines and talked vaguely about what they did, and specifically about how much they cost. Pete made encouraging sounds; I looked around. We walked around the end of the last lab bench. "And here's one of our associates. Dr. Ben Goldstein. Ben, these gentlemen from UCLA have expressed an interest in our work."

Ben saw me, and his mouth dropped open. Lots of that going around today. He shut it quickly, but he was ashen.

He was *not* pleased to see us.

Hm.

Oliver kept going, and we walked past Ben, then stopped at the bench behind him. I could still see him from this angle. Oliver was talking about the machines, and Pete was responding, carrying most of the conversation. I was trying to spend my time looking around as much as possible. Ben was still at his work station, but he was following us with his eyes. Dr. Wray was up at the front of the lab, talking to a couple of the other workers. I wondered if there were other physicians working here or if the rest of the people were lab techs.

I was studying the mechanism of a centrifuge when I heard Pete ask, "Are you treating any patients yet?"

Dr. Oliver looked very uncomfortable. "Not just yet. We're not quite to that stage. We're still working on our procedure for in vivo testing. We have some way to go before we get there."

Jeez. How many different ways were there to say no?

Dr. Wray must have overheard; she walked back to our area. "As you can imagine, it's a very big step. Our procedure is the first in what has to be a series of successful steps before we're ready to fertilize one of the ova that we've created." She smiled at us. "We're putting the finishing touches on the perfection of our procedure. We should be ready to move ahead to the next step within the next six months."

"Ah." Pete nodded sagely. "That sounds very encouraging."

He and Wray continued to chat a bit; Oliver continued to look uncomfortable. I got the impression that he really might not know much about what was going on in his own lab. Interesting.

Ben was still glowering off to the side, although he'd stopped watching us so closely.

Dr. Wray went back to her work. Dr. Oliver turned back to us. "Well, gentlemen, that's our grand tour. Is there anything else I can show you?"

He hadn't actually shown us much of anything. I now knew how much one of his machines would cost, but I didn't know anything more about his procedures than I'd learned from reading his article.

"No, thank you. This was very helpful. I understand much more now about what you're doing." Pete shook his hand.

I reached out as well. "Thank you for your time. We really appreciate it."

Dr. Oliver beamed as he showed us to the door. He certainly seemed relieved to be done with our questioning. "No trouble at all, gentlemen. If you have any more questions, Dr. Ferguson, please contact me." He gave Pete one of his cards. It was printed on top-grade paper stock. "I look forward to hearing from you."

Dr. Wray waved as we left. Ben didn't move from his stool.

We didn't say anything to each other until we were into the car. Pete locked the doors and started the engine, then looked at me. "What the *fuck*? You'd *met* her?"

"I had no idea who she was on Monday. We didn't exchange names. She said she usually swam at lunch, and she gave the same reason to Oliver today that she'd given to me on Monday. How could that be a setup?"

Pete looked out the windshield, shaking his head. "I don't know. But I don't like coincidences."

"I know, I don't either. But there aren't that many public pools in West LA; maybe she lives nearby and she really *does* swim at lunch on a regular basis."

"Maybe." Pete shook his head again. "What did you think of the tour?"

"I think Oliver talked a lot and didn't say very much. And he looked very uncomfortable when you started asking about treating patients."

"Yeah, he did." Pete pulled out of the parking lot and pointed the Jeep in the direction of UCLA. "He may have thought that I wouldn't have been as eager to give money if they weren't ready to produce any tangible results. Tangible results being babies."

"Maybe. I also thought that Ben Goldstein was unhappy to see us."

"Oh, yeah. *Very* unhappy. The only one that was cool with it, and the most forthcoming, was Dr. Wray."

"Yeah. She also seemed to be the one who really knows what's going on in the lab."

"That's probably how they divide up the work. Oliver takes care of the fundraising and Wray takes care of the lab."

"Mm hm." I thought for a minute. "I wonder what Goldstein's role is? He didn't move from his workstation while we were there, but it didn't seem like Oliver or Wray expected him to."

Pete shrugged. "He seemed to me to be just another employee."

"Yeah, maybe. He's the link to Dan, though. I'm not comfortable with that."

"Me either."

My follow up appointment with my primary care doctor was at 11:00. Pete pulled up to the entrance to the medical plaza at 10:30. "How about I meet you for dinner?"

"I have class tonight, my final class meeting. It starts at 5:30."

"Okay, then say 4:30? That'll give us plenty of time to get something on campus."

"Sounds good." I smiled at him. "Thanks for all this. I really appreciate it."

"Don't mention it. I'll see you at 4:30." Pete drove off in plenty of time to get to his 11:15 class.

I got called back to the exam room about fifteen minutes after my scheduled appointment. Dr. Weikal came in almost immediately. He asked me how I was feeling, ran my lung function tests, listened to my chest. He pronounced me nicely improved from Monday and told me to keep taking the medications and taking steamy showers and staying away from irritants. He had me schedule another appointment for a week from today, when I would have been off the steroid pills for a couple of days.

It was nearly noon, and I was hungrier than usual – a side effect of the steroids. I stopped at the student center to get a sandwich and took it back to my office to eat. As I ate, I sent Dr. Loomis my sick leave forms for Monday, yesterday and this morning, and sorted through the mail. I finished just in time to meet Liz at the reference desk.

At 1:30, Clinton arrived. Liz said, "Hi, Clinton."

"The word of the day is *bathetic*." He bowed and walked away.

"That one sounds familiar." Liz looked it up. "I thought so. Displaying insincere emotion."

Heh. Kind of like Dr. Oliver this morning, pretending to be so pleased to see us. All he'd really wanted was Pete's money.

After reference, there was nothing on my calendar. I decided to try to finish up the unscrambling of the Welsh article.

I started putting the sentences together. It was slow going. It took me nearly a half hour to get through the review of literature. As I'd noted with the methodology, a lot of the terminology and phrases seemed similar to the ones in Oliver's article. It still didn't strike me as unusual.

Until I got to the results section.

I'd paid close attention to the results section of Oliver's article. Even though I didn't understand some of the terminology, I thought I had the basic idea of what had been done and how it had turned out.

And the results section of the Welsh article sounded a *lot* like the one from Oliver's article.

But how was that possible? One procedure hadn't worked, one had. How could the results section be similar?

I had to make sure. I pulled my copy of Oliver's article out of my computer bag, and opened it to the results section.

Not only were they similar, they matched word for word. The only difference was that the negative terms had been removed. All the "did nots" had been changed to "dids." All the "did not reacts" had been changed to "reacted with."

I was astounded. It occurred to me that I'd never thought to check the references page for a citation of the Welsh article. I flipped to the back of Oliver's article. There was no citation for Hughes and Llewellyn.

I turned to the front of Oliver's article and paged up the screen to the top of the Welsh article, and started comparing. The abstract, like the results section, was identical to Oliver's article, with the negatives removed. The introductions, reviews of literature, and methodologies were identical, period. The statistics were different - but no, they'd used the same numbers. They'd just juggled the stats, using a higher value of *p*, to make them match the results they wanted.

The only section that was different was the discussion. Oliver and the others must have had to rewrite that section. Everything else, they had lifted from Hughes and Llewellyn.

Oliver's breakthrough article was completely plagiarized.

Holy. Fucking. Shit.

"Holy fucking *shit*."

"Excuse me?" I looked up. Pete was standing in the doorway. Was it 4:30 already? It was.

"Sorry. I just figured it out. The entire second article is plagiarized."

"*What*?"

"They *stole* it. Oliver and the others stole the Welsh article word for word. I wonder if the procedure even works. The numbers are the same. They just doctored them, like you said, to make them fit the results they wanted."

"So what does that mean?"

"One thing it means is that these guys have built this very lucrative lab on the basis of stolen research. If the procedure works, then the least they're guilty of is blatant plagiarism. If it doesn't work, then... I guess we're talking about fraud. Although I have no idea what laws they might have broken."

"What are you going to do?"

"I don't know. I guess there's some medical board that would handle things like this."

"Well, you can think while we eat. In the mood for pizza? I was thinking 800 Degrees."

800 Degrees was just off campus, so I could make it back to my class by 5:30. We ordered a large pepperoni and mushroom to share. We got our drinks and found a seat, and Pete jumped back into the discussion.

"This plagiarism must be what Dan stumbled across."

"Yeah. I wonder what tipped him off? Must have been something Goldstein said at some point."

"Do you think Goldstein was in on the plagiarism?"

"His name's on the article. Although if he didn't know about the first article, he may not have realized. But I don't know if that's a good enough excuse."

"There's probably a way to report something to the California medical board online. You may even be able to do it anonymously."

"Anonymous would be good."

"Yeah." Pete considered. "You might want to call HALT."

"HALT?"

"The LA County Health Authority Law Enforcement Task Force. They investigate anything having to do with fraudulent medical practice in the county."

I said, "I need to find out if all of them were in on it, though. I don't want to accuse anyone falsely."

"You could just report them all and let the medical board sort it out."

"Yeah, but if I can find out which of them was responsible…"

"Do you have any thoughts along those lines?"

"My initial thought would be Oliver. He's the first author, and I know that he worked in Cambridge at the same time that the authors of the Welsh article had their lab in Oxford. And he's the one that came to see me at the library, which was very odd. I can see Dan's boyfriend being involved, too. He must have said something to Dan to raise Dan's curiosity in the first place, right? The woman – Dr. Wray – I don't know. She co-founded the lab with Oliver, but she may not have known about the earlier research."

Pete frowned. "I don't see how any of them could not know. But the ones who were acting squirrely when we were there this morning were Oliver and Goldstein. Wray, on the other hand, seemed *very* pleasantly surprised to see you. Not the reaction I'd expect from a criminal."

"Right. Oliver's my first choice for chief perpetrator."

"Agreed." Pete speared a black olive from my plate. "What's your next move?"

"I don't know. I need to mull this over for a while."

"Okay. Do you want me to pick you up after class?"

"Nah. I'll ride the bus. I'm gonna let them out early tonight."

I went to my classroom, then opened my laptop and found the website for the Medical Board of California and their Consumer Complaint form. There was a section to report fraud or other "unprofessional conduct." I bookmarked it but didn't fill it in. It wasn't anonymous, and I kept thinking that there might be an innocent explanation for what I'd found.

Not that I could conjure one up.

Even though it was early, I was getting tired. The students arrived, and I gave them their final in-class assignments. Each of them had a different complicated history reference question to answer, which they would write up and turn in by the end of class. I told them that I'd decided that they didn't have to present their findings tonight. As soon as each one was finished, they could leave and turn in their reports online by tomorrow morning. They were delighted to hear that and jumped right in to work. The last one was done and out the door by 8:15. I packed up and headed for the bus stop.

It was dusk, but not completely dark. I was thinking while I walked and not paying attention to anything around me. That was my mistake.

I was in the shadows, about halfway between the library and the bus stop, when someone bumped into me from behind. I turned, a little off balance, and got sucker punched. I staggered, and someone else grabbed me from behind.

There were two of them. The first guy punched me again in the side of the head, then in the gut. I folded, and the second guy grabbed my computer bag and tossed it out of the way. The first guy then proceeded to hit me five or six times, mostly in the face, once more in the gut. I tasted blood and went down. I heard running steps, then silence.

It all took about ten seconds. Neither one of them had said a word.

I rolled to my side and sat up. Blood was streaming down my face, my jaw felt out of place, and my eyes were rapidly swelling. I pulled my phone out of my pocket and called 911.

It didn't take long for the UCLA police - Officer Don Greene - and EMTs to get to me. As soon as I told Greene what had happened, he took off in the direction I thought my assailants had run. The EMTs picked me up off the ground and set me on the back of the ambulance. They made me answer some questions - name, rank, and serial number, who was the president, what day was it, that kind of thing. Then they started mopping up the blood. I had a fat lip, cuts on both cheekbones and above my left eye, a bloody nose, and a pair of rapidly developing black eyes. They thought I should get an X-ray of my jaw, but I didn't want to go to the hospital. The EMTs put a couple of butterfly bandages on my face and gave me two ice packs. I needed three, but I only had two hands. By the time they'd accomplished all that, Officer Greene was back.

"Are you an employee of the university, sir?"

I nodded. "Lib'ry." Oh, it hurt to talk.

"Okay. What happened here?"

I steeled myself to try to form words. "Mugged." It came out more like "mm-ugggd."

"Mugged? By who?"

I shrugged and held up two fingers.

"Two? Men?"

"Mm hm."

"Did you get a look at them?"

"Unh unh. Ski masks." It came out "ssski musk."

"Ski masks. What else were they wearing?"

"Black. Gloves." *Gluffs*.

"Could you see any identifying characteristics? Race, height, weight?"

"Bod' whi'. Saw arms." I indicated the space right above my wrists.

"Okay. What size guys were they?"

"Big. One daller, one shorder but beefy."

"Which direction did they go?"

I pointed to the east. "Off campus."

Greene grimaced and got on his radio. One of the EMTs got in front of me and ran me through some neurological tests - follow his finger with my eyes, touch his finger then my nose, reflexes. The other was trying to mop up some of the blood. "Sir, when was your last tetanus shot?"

I shrugged. He started preparing one.

Greene returned. "Did they take anything?"

"Unh unh."

"They just beat you up."

"Mm hm."

Greene paused, regarding me for a second. "Any idea who's got it in for you?"

"Unh unh." That wasn't entirely correct, but I wasn't going to go through the whole story again. It would be easier to tell Kevin's partner Tim about it.

Tim and Kevin were the next to arrive. Tim and Greene talked off to the side for a few minutes; Kevin sat down beside me on the ambulance bumper. The EMT gave me the tetanus shot and two new ice packs; Kevin took one and held it on my jaw, gently. His voice was soft. "You gonna live?"

"Mm hm." I looked over at him. "'M okay."

Kevin's eyes got damp. "You don't look okay, I have to tell you."

"D'anks so mush."

He laughed, sniffed and wiped his nose. "Dad's gonna kill me."

"F'r whu'?"

"Not keeping an eye on you. Letting this happen." He bit his lip. "I'm the big brother. I'm supposed to watch out for you."

I tried to make a face at him; I'm sure it looked suitably disgusted. And disgusting. "Not y'r day to wa'zh me."

He shook his head and put his arm around my shoulders. I leaned into him, grateful to be able to lean on something. "Gonna fi'd back."

"How's that?"

"This's psychological war. Godda get me a psychologis'."

Kevin's gaze shot over to me. "Oh yeah? You got one in mind?"

"Mm hm."

Kevin grinned. "I like that."

Tim finished up with Greene and came over. His expression was grim. "Are you okay?"

"Mm hm. More 'r less."

Tim looked from me to Kevin and back, shaking his head. "Okay. Here's what I got from Officer Greene. Two guys jumped you, wearing black and ski masks, beat you up and ran off without taking anything. Both white, one taller than you and one shorter, the shorter one a beefy guy. That sound right?"

"'Zackly."

"Okay, good. Did you notice them before they jumped you?"

"Unh unh. Not payin' 'denshun."

"And you're sure they didn't take anything."

"Unh unh. Dropped my bag, id's ri'd there."

Tim picked up my bag and brought it over. "Your laptop's still here. Still got your phone? Your wallet?"

"In my pockeds."

Tim checked to make sure. "Okay. So you think this must be related to all the other stuff that's been happening?"

"Mus' be, righ'?"

"That would be my thought." Tim closed his notebook and slapped it against his thigh, thinking. "I think our best bet is to find out who's been sabotaging your computer. That may lead us to everyone else. I'm going to have a talk with the computer crimes detective tomorrow."

"Inside job."

"Most likely. Who's been in your office?"

"Just ID guy. Andy Mi'shell. Bud dey can condrol nedwork remodely. Could be anybody."

"Right. But I'll take a look at this Andy first."

I sighed. All of a sudden I was exhausted. "Sounds good."

"Okay." Tim turned to the EMTs. "You guys all done?"

"Yes, if he's not going to let us transport him." The EMT who had bandaged my face handed me a sheet of paper. "I need you to sign this, which says we recommended transport and you refused." I signed. He handed me another sheet of paper. "Here are instructions. Be sure to read them. If you have any change in consciousness, any blurred vision..."

"Yeah, yeah, I'll come in." I stood up, with Kevin still propping me, and looked at Tim. "You guys dakin' me home?"

"Yeah. We'll drive you down to Pete's on the way to the station. Did you call him?"

"Unh unh."

"Well." Kevin raised his eyebrows. "He's in for an unpleasant surprise."

We pulled up at the townhouse about 15 minutes later. I could barely see out of my left eye. Kevin dug through my bag and handed me my keys, and I opened the door. Pete wasn't in bed, as I had hoped; he was up, on the sofa, surrounded by books and papers. When he saw us he stood up, then his jaw dropped when he saw my face.

"Oh my God! Oh my God. What the hell happened to you?"

My jaw was really throbbing. It was getting harder to talk, not easier. "God 'ugged."

Kevin said, "He was assaulted walking to the bus stop from the library. Two guys, one held him and the other one hit him. They didn't steal anything. You got an ice pack?"

Pete stared at me for a second then went into action. "Yeah. Two of them, I'd say." He ran up the stairs to the fridge and came right back with two bags of frozen peas and two dish towels. I sank down onto the love seat. My head hurt, and it was getting harder to move, period. By tomorrow morning, I'd be a wreck.

Pete moved pillows around so I could lean back, then wrapped the peas in the towels and gently applied them to both sides of my face. I winced. "Sorry, hon. Sorry."

Some distant corner of my brain registered the word "hon," but I couldn't do anything with it right then.

Pete turned back to Kevin. "They didn't catch them?"

"No. They got off campus too fast. And they were wearing black and ski masks, so Jamie couldn't get a good description. Patrol is looking for them, but they haven't found anything yet."

Pete shook his head. "Un-fucking-believable. What is this? Sending a message? Like burning up your apartment wasn't enough? Who's doing this? And why?"

"It's got to be related to this dying request thing he's trying to solve. The timing is right. He's got to be getting close to something, but what? Even he doesn't know."

Kevin and Pete continued to dissect it out. My head was killing me. I needed Kevin to leave, or at least to be quiet. I tried to get their attention, and finally threw a pillow at Pete. It missed, but it landed between them, so they both turned to look at me.

I pointed at Kevin. "Oud." I pointed at Pete. "Drugs."

Kevin rolled his eyes, but agreed. "Okay, okay. I'll call you tomorrow. You're staying home, right?"

I gave him a thumbs up.

"All right." He turned to Pete. "Call me if you need me."

"Right." Pete watched Kevin get in his car, then locked the door and turned back to me. "One pain pill, coming up."

Since I hadn't gone to the ER, I didn't have a prescription for anything. Fortunately, Pete had some leftover oxycodone from when he'd had his wisdom teeth out several months ago. He brought me one and a glass of water with a straw, and I managed to get it down. Pete took a critical look at me, surveying the damage more dispassionately. "I'll try to get the blood out of your shirt, but it may be history."

"'S okay."

"Can you sit up? I'll get this off of you."

I sat up and scooted forward a bit, and Pete gently unbuttoned my shirt and pushed it back off my shoulders. He tossed it to the floor, turned back to me and gasped.

"Whuh?"

He was looking at my arms. "You've got bruises coming up where the guy gripped your arms to hold you."

I looked down, but I couldn't see anything. My face was getting so swollen it was hard to see at all. I pointed at my shirt, which Pete had tossed on the floor. "My only dress shird."

"Well, you won't be going anywhere for a couple of days. And you can go back to work in polo shirts. No one will care."

My face and head were starting to hurt. "Need more ice."

"Right." Pete put the bags of peas back in the freezer and came back with two bags of corn. I laid back on the sofa so that I didn't have to hold the ice. Pete arranged the bags over the dish towels. "How's that?"

"Mm hm."

"Okay. I'm going to put your shirt to soak." He went off for a few minutes. The oxycodone was starting to kick in. My head was throbbing a bit less than it had been. The ice was numbing my face. I probably could have fallen asleep right there, but Pete came back and patted me on the leg. "You've still got a lot of blood on you, down your neck and under your collar area, some down onto your chest. And in your hair. We need to get you cleaned up."

"'Kay."

"That ice has been on for ten minutes. Ten more minutes, and we'll get you into the shower. That'll be the easiest way to approach it."

"'Kay."

He went off to do something else. I just laid there. My head was too fuzzy to think about anything. After a while, I couldn't tell how long, Pete came back.

"Okay. The corn is melted. Do you think you can sit up?"

I took the bags of corn from my face and handed them to him. He took them back to the freezer, and I tried to sit up. I didn't get very far. Pete came back and slid his arm around my ribs, helping to lift me to a seated position. I grunted. My ribs and abs were getting sorer.

"Okay?" Pete rubbed my back a little.

"Mm hm." I didn't want to do or say anything that would slow my progress in getting into bed.

"Okay. Let's get your t-shirt off. I think we might as well scrap this, right? You've got more of these."

"I's bluddy?"

"Oh yeah. It's bloody." He started lifting it from the bottom and eased my arms out of it, then lifted it over my head and showed it to me. The white t-shirt was now striped brownish-red at the top and halfway down the chest.

"Ugh. Doss id."

Pete tossed it across the room, then knelt down and took off my shoes. "Okay. Can you stand up?"

"Mm hm. You help."

Pete stood up, gripped my arms just above my elbows, and lifted as I stood. I got to my feet and swayed. The oxycodone was starting to do its thing.

"Okay, good. Just stand here for a second." Pete looked at my chest and abdomen. "You're bruised all over. He punched you in the ribs and belly?"

"Mm hm."

Pete growled. "Son of a bitch." He wrapped his arms around me and held me for a minute, standing there. "We'll get them, babe. We'll get them."

"Mm hm."

He stepped back from me, still holding my shoulders. "Think you can walk upstairs?"

"Mm hm. Godda."

He smiled. "Okay, tough guy. Let's go, then." He slid his left arm around my waist and we started walking slowly. I managed to get to the stairs, but by the time I got there I was groaning out loud.

"Let's get you undressed, and we can get in the shower."

Pete gripped my belt on either side of my hips and half-pushed, half-dragged me up the stairs. We got to the master bedroom, and he propped me against the wall for a minute to get positioned, then maneuvered me in and set me down on the toilet lid. "See how far you can make it towards getting your pants off." Then he proceeded to strip down in front of me.

I'd have to be dead three days to not appreciate the sight of Pete taking his clothes off. Unfortunately, at the moment, I couldn't do much to express my appreciation. I tried, though. "Mmmm hmmmm."

He looked at me and laughed. "You're insatiable, you know that?"

I made a sound of some sort. He laughed again and reached out. "Come on. Let's get you cleaned up."

I stood up and leaned on him while he got my pants down and I kicked them away. Then he helped me into the shower and turned it on. The water felt wonderful, as long as it didn't get near my face. Pete washed the rest of the blood from my neck, shoulders and chest, then did a quick wash of the rest of me. He sat me down to work the shampoo through my hair. It really stung when we rinsed it out, hitting the cuts on my face. I was dizzy and still in pain, although my jaw and head had settled down to a dull throb.

In spite of that, my close proximity to Pete resulted in a physical response. Not as vigorous as it would have been under normal circumstances, for sure, but a definite sign that I wasn't quite dead yet.

But I wasn't able to do anything about it, and by the time we were out of the shower and dried off, I was too buzzed on the oxycodone to maintain my interest, so to speak.

Pete got me situated in bed, then helped me into a pair of my new pajama pants. It was easier lying down. Then he slid in beside me. "How ya doin'?"

I tried to smile at him. "Da'ks."

"You're welcome." He kissed me on the forehead. "Think you can sleep?"

"Ma'be. Gon' dry."

"Okay. Me too." He turned out the light. "Wake me up if you need anything."

"Mm hm."

Pete stretched out beside me, touching just enough to provide warmth. His breathing evened out and slowed down into his sleep pattern quickly. I wasn't sure if I could fall asleep or not, in spite of the drug effects. But I was still wondering about it when I did slide into unconsciousness.

I was dreaming that I was watching Pete get a tattoo when something woke me up. Pete's arm was draped over my chest but he was awake too. A very slight tinkling sound followed. It sounded an awful lot like broken glass being brushed away.

Pete breathed "shhhh" into my ear. Then another broken glass sound. Pete whispered, "Shotgun under bed. Loaded. Not chambered. Safety on." Then he rolled away, to a standing position, and silently slid his bedside table drawer open. He lifted out his old service weapon and laid it on the top of the table. He pulled on a pair of sweatpants, picked the gun back up, and eased the bedroom door open.

I rolled stiffly to the side of the bed. Every movement was painful, but my adrenalin was flowing so fast that the pain didn't fully reach my consciousness.

I crouched to the floor, holding on to the bed. The shotgun was within reach, and I lifted it, then stood. I couldn't hear anything from downstairs. Pete was still standing with the bedroom door cracked. He waved me over. "Stay behind me. Silent. Stay out of the light." I nodded. He opened the bedroom door all the way and stepped out into the hallway.

Pete crept down the stairs and stopped at the next to last step before the landing. I followed him, staying about two steps behind. He quickly looked around the wall. Now I could hear movement. It sounded like only one person, but I wasn't sure. The switch to turn on the living room ceiling light was on the opposite side of the wall from us. Pete leaned back to me and breathed into my ear again. "When I say, rack the gun. Then I'll turn on the light."

I nodded. He edged around the wall and motioned me over to the kitchen counter, where I could look down into the living room. Now I could see a little by the street light that was filtering into the living room through the hole in the living room window. There was only one guy. He was going through the papers on the ottoman, holding a small flashlight in his teeth as he examined each one. I smiled grimly to myself. If he was looking for the Welsh article, he was out of luck. I'd never printed it.

The rustling of the papers was making enough noise that the guy apparently hadn't heard us approach at all. I raised the shotgun, ready. Pete whispered, "Now."

I racked the gun. The guy dropped his flashlight and yelled, "Shit! Don't shoot!"

Pete flipped the light on. "Hands up! Get on your knees! On the floor! Down! Now! Hands behind your head!" He charged down the stairs, gun in front of him. "Get the fuck down on the fucking floor right now! On your face! Hands behind your head!"

I followed him down the stairs, shotgun tucked against my shoulder. The burglar was on the floor, repeating like a mantra, "Don'tshootme don'tshootme don'tshootme..."

Pete reached him. "Shut up. If you piss on my floor, I will shoot you."

“Okay! Okay!” The guy did sound terrified. Pete looked up at me. “Get the duct tape. It’s in the ottoman.”

Who keeps duct tape in their ottoman? But there it was. “Tear off some pieces. Keep them coming.” I handed the first one to Pete. He taped the guy’s fingers together first, then pulled the guy’s hands behind his back and taped his wrists together. Then his ankles, then he rolled the guy over.

“You recognize this guy?”

“Unh unh. Bud c’odes same.”

“How about that.” Pete stood back, but kept the Glock aimed at the guy. I didn’t lower the shotgun either. He looked over at me and grinned. “Nice work, pardner. Call 911 and we’ll get this turkey roasted.”

I laughed. This was nuts. I got the phone and dialed.

It only took the Santa Monica police about three minutes to get to the house. In that three minutes, the guy kept babbling, and Pete kept telling him to shut up. He sure looked like the bulkier of the two guys who had attacked me. Pete had the door open when the police arrived, and they promptly arrested the guy. He’d broken the window with a tire iron, but had left it outside. Not a very good burglar.

The Santa Monica cops heard the story, then called West LA. Tim and a detective named Pinter arrived and discussed jurisdiction with the Santa Monica cops for a while, then hauled the guy away after everyone took statements from Pete and me. Pete called his insurance company and the Santa Monica police gave him the name of someone to call to board up the window. They stayed until he arrived. The window was boarded up, the house was secured, and everyone left. It was 4:30 am.

Chapter 10
Thursday, June 7

When I woke up again, it was 9:30. I could hear muffled voices coming from downstairs. I didn't want to move, but my bladder wouldn't take no for an answer. I rolled to my side and groaned at the ache in my abs. I laid in that position for a minute, waiting for the ache to fade. When it did, I swung my legs off the bed and pushed myself into a sitting position.

Shit. Everything hurt. My head started throbbing again, and I realized that I could barely see. My left eye was swollen shut and my right was narrowed to a slit. My whole face hurt in addition to the pain in my head, and my left arm ached from the tetanus shot. I held onto the nightstand as I put my weight on my feet, then straightened up. Now I was dizzy too. Great. I stood still for a minute until the dizziness passed, then staggered into the bathroom.

When I went downstairs, Tim, Kevin, and Pete were all in the living room, drinking coffee and talking. They looked up as I eased myself downstairs.

Pete said, "Oh my *God.*"

Kevin gasped. Tim said, "You look like shit."

I still couldn't open my jaw much. "Danks. I'm 'ware of dad."

Pete stood up as I sat. "Can you eat anything? Do you need a pain pill?"

"Unh unh 'n' mm hm."

"I'm gonna make you a milkshake." He ran up to the kitchen and returned with a glass of water, a straw, and an oxycodone. I swallowed the pill. Pete headed back up the stairs and started banging around in the kitchen.

Tim said, "We were just filling Pete in on our perp. When the guy found out he'd committed felony assault on a cop's brother, he nearly pissed his pants. He told us everything he knows, which wasn't much."

“He was one dad hid me?”

Kevin said, “No. He was the guy who held you back while the second guy hit you. He’s a small-time burglar with a long sheet, and he was also the guy who broke into our place.”

Tim continued. “He was hired by the guy who hit you. He only knows the guy’s first name, which is Ed. Maybe. And he doesn’t know who hired Ed, although he knows someone did. Ed was following someone else’s orders.”

Kevin laughed. “He’s in the running for dumbest criminal of the year. He was supposed to take your computer bag with him when they ran off after beating you up. He had to come back here because he’d left it behind.”

Pete appeared with a huge glass full of chocolate shake. I stuck my straw in and took a sip. It was heavenly. “Danks. So good.”

Pete sat down next to me. “I called your supervisor this morning and told her what happened. She was appropriately horrified and said to take as much time as you need.”

“Mmf. I forgod ‘boud work.”

“I had to call in for myself, so it occurred to me to call in for you, too.” He settled back and gestured to Tim. “Go on.”

“There’s not much else to it. He couldn’t give us a better description than you had of this Ed guy. White, medium height, medium build, brown hair, no scars, marks or tattoos that he could see. He did swear that he didn’t know anything about messing with your office or computer, and I believe him. This guy’s not smart enough to be a hacker.”

Kevin looked grim. “So we’re not much further along now than we were.”

“But we’ve made a little progress. And that’s better than nothing, which is what we had before.” Tim stood up. “I’m going to take some pictures of you, if you don’t mind, while you look your worst. We can use them as evidence in our case against this guy’s accomplice when we find him.”

I shrugged. “‘Kay.”

He took several pictures of my face from every angle imaginable. He also took pictures of the bruises on my abs and ribs, which had bloomed up nicely. He finished and stepped back. "The robbery guys are still talking to our bad guy, but I don't think there's anything else he can tell us. But if there is, I'll let you know." He smiled at me sympathetically. "We'll figure all this out. No worries."

Kevin reached out and hugged me gently. "Please behave. Do what Pete tells you to do. Okay? Please?"

"Mm hm. Don' dell Dad."

"Oh, hell no. I'll tell him we got the guy that broke into our place, and that's all." Kevin stepped back, but kept his hands on my shoulders. "I'll talk to you later."

"'Kay."

We saw them off. I sank back down onto the sofa and picked up my shake. The oxycodone was starting to help, and my head wasn't pounding as hard.

Pete sat down with me. "They're coming to fix the window this afternoon." He brushed my hair back from my forehead. "You really do look awful. I'm going to clean up the kitchen." He went up the stairs.

I drank more shake and set it on the ottoman, within reach. I leaned back and was overcome with a wave of emotion and exhaustion. I was beaten. They, whoever *they* were, had beaten me up, burned all my stuff, hacked my computer, and disabled my car. They'd succeeded in disabling me. I'd thought it was an intellectual puzzle that I could handle on my own. I was wrong.

The pain was messing with my emotions. Tears started leaking out of my eyes and running across the cuts on my cheekbones. It stung.

"Ow."

Pete had gone into the kitchen when Kevin and Tim had left. Now he looked down at me and didn't like what he saw. He hurried down the stairs and sat down next to me. "What's wrong?"

"Everyding." I lifted my t-shirt to dab at my eyes. "Ow."

Pete didn't say anything. He scooted over and wrapped his arms around me.

Oh my God. I needed this. I needed him. I cried harder. It hurt my ribs and abs, too. "Ow, ow, ow."

To his credit, Pete didn't laugh. He just hugged me and rubbed my back. It was soothing. I calmed down a little bit and tried to regroup. "Sorry."

"It's okay." Pete moved back a bit and pulled a tissue from the box on the ottoman, then started patting my face gently, drying it. "Everything you've been through, you deserve a good cry. Most guys would have been on their knees long before this."

"Huh." I took the tissue from him and wiped my nose. "Don' know 'boud dad."

"I do." Pete brushed my hair off my forehead. "You're a tough guy. You come from a family of tough guys. There isn't anyone I'd rather have at my back in any situation than you. Or Kevin."

I shook my head. "'M nod Kebin."

Pete smiled. "No, you're not, and thank God for that, right?"

I laughed a little and shook my head again.

"Really." Pete was serious again. "Kevin's bigger than you, and he's obviously been trained as a cop, but you and he are made out of the same stuff. The right stuff, if you want to coin a phrase."

I leaned back and sighed. "'D he ever dell you 'boud our name?"

"Nope. What about it?"

"Brodie. Comes from Bridei." I spelled it for him. "Kings of the Pic's in Scodlan'. Warriors."

Pete grinned. "I'm not surprised. Warrior kings, eh? Very cool."

I sniffled a little.

"And their California descendants are warriors, too, right? Warriors for truth and justice."

"Heh." I looked away from him. "But dis dime id's nod workin'."

"Sure it is." Pete handed me the milkshake I'd abandoned on the ottoman. "You've uncovered the truth. Justice is going to take a little longer this time, that's all. But we'll get it. We'll get them, whoever *them* is."

I looked back at him. "You dink?"

"Yes. Because now we know what they're trying to hide." Pete smiled at me again. "But we're not going to do it today, right?"

I shook my head. "Need do do somedhin' else today."

Pete frowned. "You are not going anywhere or doing anything. You're going to sit here and drink milkshakes and take naps. End of discussion."

"Nod somedhin' like dad." I looked at him, at this guy that I needed. He wanted me at his back; I needed him at mine. "'Boud us."

Pete looked wary. "As in... *Us?*"

"Mm hm." I took his hand. "Been 'dupid. Dryin' to be 'lone. Not leddin' anyone close. Afraid of you."

That surprised him. "Afraid of me? Why the hell would you be afraid of me?"

I swallowed. "Only one able to hurd me."

His surprised expression melted into sadness. "Oh, Jamie. I would never do that. I would never..." He sniffed a little himself. "When we were together before, it was the best time of my life. But you weren't in the same place then, and then Luke reappeared - and it seemed like you were pulling away from me, and I felt like I owed it to Luke to give that relationship another try. But when that didn't work, I didn't want anyone else - just you. I guess I've been waiting for you to come to your senses..." He laughed a little. "I wish it hadn't taken a major disaster for that to happen, but I'll take what I can get."

I shook my head. "Didn' want to get hurd. Didn' wanna need anyone. First time wid you I was fallin' for you doo and god afraid.

W'en Luke came back id solved da' for me. Daded a lot of od'er people to nod dink 'boud you." I looked at his hand, holding mine. It looked right.

I leaned back on the pillows. "Sorry for bein' so s'ubborn. Wasdin' so mush dime."

Pete stroked the palm of my hand with his thumb. It was weirdly soothing. "No apology necessary. As soon as you can move again, we're gonna make up for lost time."

I laughed, and it hurt. "Ow."

That made him smile. He let go of my hand and got up. "Time for more drugs for you." He checked my glass. "And a fresh milkshake." He went to the kitchen.

In spite of my injuries, I felt lucky. I'd been given a second chance. Now I just had to make sure I didn't mess it up.

At some point in the early afternoon, Pete got a call and spent several minutes on the phone, mostly saying "Yeah" and "Okay" and "Huh." When he hung up, he told me, "We've got a summit meeting tomorrow morning at West LA Division. Tim, Kevin, your UCLA computer crimes guy, a couple of Wilshire detectives, and the LAPD liaison to HALT. They haven't gotten anything else out of the guy who broke in here, and they believe that he doesn't know anything else. Still no idea who his accomplice was. The UCLA cop - what's his name?"

"Roger Blake."

"Right, Blake. He and the head of your IT department were able to figure out who was sabotaging your computer."

That made me sit up and take notice. "Whoa. Who was id?"

"The guy who was supposedly fixing the computer. Andy Mitchell."

My jaw dropped, even though it hurt. "You're shidding me."

"Nope. He's said he was paid to do it, but he's lawyered up and won't say anything about who paid him or why."

"D'ad's jus' bizarre." I couldn't believe it. "I can' believe id."

"I know. I'm not sure how they figured it out, I guess they'll say tomorrow. Tim did say that Andy installed a keystroke logger on your computer the first time he was in your office supposedly fixing it. From that, they were able to tell what your friend Diane was doing on your computer."

"Wha'?"

"Snooping in your email. The West Hollywood sheriff's deputies picked her up early this morning. UCLA is going to charge her with unauthorized access to the university network, or something like that."

"Oh my God. She'll lose her zhob."

"Maybe. She should have thought of that before she got stupid."

"Yeah." I was having trouble dredging up much sympathy for Diane. "She owes me a 'pology."

"Big time."

Talking about email made me think of checking mine. I found only one message of interest.

An email from Ben Goldstein.

Dr. Brodie,

I have come across a note that Dan left for me in which he suggests that you might be able to help me answer some of the questions that he left for me. I would like to meet with you in person, at a place of your choosing. Please.

Thank you,

Ben Goldstein

I showed it to Pete. "Whad do you dink?"

"Well, he did say please." Pete frowned. "It sounds like he's worried about something. He may be innocent in this and trying to figure out what's going on himself."

"Do you dink I should dalk to him?"

"I think *we* should talk to him. You're not doing anything by yourself that's remotely related to your fraud case."

I nodded. I would have argued with him if I'd been healthy, but... "Where?"

"Here."

I was surprised. "But den he'll know where we live. If he's one of de bad guys."

Pete laughed. "If he's one of the bad guys, he already knows where we live."

True.

"Okay. Dis evening?"

"Sure."

Ben's phone number was at the bottom of his email. I called him. He said, "What's wrong with your voice?"

"I got socked in de jaw las' nighd. S'ill hurds do dalk."

"Wow." He paused. "I don't want to talk about any of this on the phone, or anywhere near my office. Can I come to your place?"

I gave him directions. If he did already know where we lived, he was doing a good job of acting like he didn't. I hung up and looked at Pete. "Seben o'clock."

I spent the rest of the day alternating between dozing, drinking soup and milkshakes, and watching old movies. Pete alternated between doing laundry, fixing me soup and milkshakes, and grading papers. At precisely 7:00, the doorbell rang.

Pete answered the door. Ben was still wearing an expensive suit, but his tie was askew and he looked rumpled and tired. He introduced himself to Pete, then came in and got his first glimpse of my face. "Holy mother of God! You didn't just get socked in the jaw!"

I shook my head.

"What the hell happened?"

Pete gave him a severely abridged version. Ben couldn't stop staring. If he was faking surprise, he was doing a fabulous job. He sat on the chair next to the new window; Pete sat down on the sofa next to me. Pete started the conversation. "So, Dan left you a note."

"Yeah." Ben looked at Pete and me sitting next to each other. "Are you two a couple?"

Pete waited for me to answer; I felt him tense up a bit. I nodded. "Mm hm."

Pete relaxed. I could almost feel him smile.

Ben stood up and handed me a folded sheet of paper, then sat back down. The handwriting was Dan's. I unfolded it and read.

Dear Ben,

If you find this, then I'm gone. I'm so sorry. If I had known where this would lead, I would have approached it far differently.

Take this to a guy named Jamie Brodie, who's a librarian at UCLA. He's been working on a problem for me. He'll tell you what this is and why you need to know about it. Then you'll have to decide what to do about it.

All my love forever,

Dan

Underneath the signature was the citation for the Welsh article, in Welsh.

I handed the note back to Ben. He folded it carefully and put it back in his jacket pocket. "Do you know what that means?"

I nodded. "Do you remember de firs' ardicle you wrode wi' Oliver and Wray?"

"Sure."

I leaned over and handed him my laptop, with the translation of the Welsh article open on the screen. "Read dis."

He started reading. His eyes got bigger as he went. He stopped reading and started scrolling through pages, reading bits and pieces. "This is..." He looked up at me, aghast. "This is our article, word for word."

Pete took over. "The only thing that's different is the statistical section, and it's only different because your article used a higher *p* value than Hughes and Llewellyn did."

"I did the stats for this article." Ben seemed to be in mild shock. "They gave me the numbers and told me what *p* values to use." He looked up, his eyes wide. "I didn't do any of the research on this article. They told me they'd list me as an author if I ran the stats for them. It was my first publication."

Pete asked, "Who gave you the numbers? Both Wray and Oliver?"

"No. It was Dr. Oliver." The full force of the discovery hit Ben. "So our article is plagiarized from this one? Word for word?"

"It seems that way."

Ben was dazed for a moment, then looked back up at us. "Tell me how you found out about this."

Pete told him the whole story, from my receipt of Dan's letter to last night's break-in. "Frankly, we weren't sure you weren't involved."

Ben was angry, but not at us. "Oh, no. Fuck, no." He got up and started pacing, then turned back to us. "So someone killed Danny because he found this out?"

"We think so."

Ben looked at me. "Why did he ask you to find out about this?"

"I dink because he knew me well enough to know I'd dig undil I god de answer."

Ben started pacing again. "I thought from the beginning it wasn't right that Dan died from a seizure. He hadn't had a seizure in the two years I'd known him. And he never missed his meds. Never. If we were out someplace at the time he was supposed to take them, we'd have to leave right then. I got his autopsy report myself, but since it didn't show anything else..." He stopped to think. "Since it didn't show anything else, then how did he die?"

Pete mused. "Hard to say. When I was a cop, I talked to the coroner about that once. He said there were ways to kill people and leave no trace, usually with an injection of some kind. He mentioned potassium and a couple of other things."

Ben sat back down. He looked deflated and ten years older. "My employer killed my boyfriend. Or had him killed. Unbelievable." He shook his head. "Oliver is all about the kindly mentor image, the rich uncle who wants to make your life as comfortable as possible. It's just hard to imagine him being responsible for this."

"Is there any way it could be Dr. Wray?"

Ben rubbed his eyes. "I don't see how. She didn't even know Dan. And you tell me that Oliver was at Cambridge when these Welsh guys were at Oxford... It has to be him, right?"

Pete shrugged. "It seems to be pointing that way."

Ben leaned back in the chair and huffed out a breath. "Well." He stared into space for a minute, then looked back at us. "What are you going to do about this?"

"There's a task force connected to LAPD that deals with fraudulent medical practice. We figured we'd start with them. Let them take the investigation from here."

Ben nodded. "Okay." He looked at his watch and stood up. "I have to be on my way. I have some unfinished work at the lab. And then I have to get my CV updated and start looking for a new job." He shook our hands. "If you think I can help you in any other way, please let me know."

Pete nodded. "We will. But you'll probably be hearing from the LAPD within the next couple of days."

"All right." He looked back at us solemnly. "Thank you. I mean that. And thank you for being someone Dan knew he could count on."

My voice failed me at that, but I nodded. Pete saw Ben out, closed and locked the door and turned back to me. "He doesn't know you and Dan had a history."

"He doesn' need do know. Doesn' madder."

"True." Pete sat back down beside me. "It's still looking like Oliver is our guy, huh?"

"Yeah. If Ben was involved, he's in de wrong business. He needs a Hollywood agen'. And Dan didn' suspec' him."

Pete nodded. "I believe him. But we still don't know about Dr. Wray."

"Dere's nod'ing poinding ad her. Id's all Oliver."

"Yeah." Pete sighed. "Well. We'll see what happens at our summit meeting tomorrow." He looked at me closely. "You look worn out. Ready for bed?"

"Yep."

We took another hot shower and went to bed.

Chapter 11
Friday, June 8

The next morning I woke up later than usual, in spite of going to bed earlier than usual. Before I moved, I surveyed my body parts. My head pounding had devolved to a dull ache; that was an improvement. I opened my jaw a bit; it seemed that I had a little more motion than I had yesterday. My muscles were still sore, but not quite as stiff as they had been. It was good to see a little progress.

Pete was already up; I could hear him rattling around downstairs. I got up slowly and made my way to the bathroom. I figured another hot shower might loosen me up even more, and it did. I got dressed in jeans and a polo shirt and went downstairs. Pete was in the kitchen; he met me on the landing and gave me a hug, then stood back and surveyed my face. "You still look terrible."

I smiled as sweetly as I could and gave him the finger.

He laughed. "Are you feeling better?"

"A little. Not as stiff. And I can make t's."

"Good. I'm impatient with not being able to kiss you. Are you up to chewing food yet?"

"Don't think so."

"Okay. Want another milkshake?"

Yes, I did.

Near 10:00, we drove up to the West LA station, went in, and got our visitor IDs. Pete stopped to say hello to a few people along the way; this was his former workplace. We made our way to the detectives' area and were ushered into a small conference room.

Roger Blake was horrified to see my face; I explained quickly what had happened. Tim introduced us to Steve Ringland and John Kaliszuk, the Wilshire detectives; they were there because Cedars was in their territory, and Dan had died there. The HALT liaison was a woman named Sherlene Passey. Kevin was squeezed into a corner, looking glum. I made a "what?" face at him, and he shrugged. Nothing major, then.

We got settled at the table. Tim stood up at a whiteboard and laid out the timeline of the case for everyone: Dan's death, his letter to me, my request of the articles and the ensuing sabotage of my computer, my visit to Dan's office and the slashing of my tires in the Cedars parking lot, my being followed, the attempted break in at my apartment, Dan's autopsy results, the break in and fire at my apartment, the hacking of my medical records, my discovery of the plagiarism, my beating, and the break in at the townhouse. The Wilshire guys were taking notes.

"So, we've got two of the perpetrators." Tim started a new list on the other side of the board. "Mauro Politano is the guy who broke in to both Jamie's apartment and Pete's townhouse. He's got a longish sheet, mostly burglary and petty theft. The apartment was his first arson. He did both the apartment and the townhouse burglaries alone. He's also one of the two guys that beat Jamie up."

Everyone turned to look at my face again; I rolled my eyes.

"He's the one that held Jamie's arms, not the one who did the punching. Politano has told us that he was hired by the guy who did the punching, whose first name is supposedly Ed. He gave us a description, which is too generic to be of use. We've had him looking at mug shots, but so far nothing. We do believe he's telling us everything he knows."

Tim turned back to the board and wrote Andy Mitchell beneath Politano's name. "Andy Mitchell is the UCLA employee who sabotaged Jamie's computer. He told us he was paid to do the job, but won't tell us anything else. He did say that he didn't know anything about the other crimes, but I'm not to the point where I believe what he says yet. We're working with his attorney to try to make a deal, but right now it doesn't look good. I get the feeling he's protecting someone, but he won't say."

Tim paused for a couple of mouthfuls of coffee. I raised my hand.

"Yeah, Jamie?"

"We had a visit yesterday." I pointed to Pete, who recounted the entire conversation we'd had with Ben.

"Holy *shit*." Tim turned back to the board. "Okay. So Goldstein thinks that Tristan Oliver stole the original article, and that Dan stumbled across the plagiarism and might have been threatening to expose Oliver. But why would Oliver kill him? Why wouldn't he just pay him off?"

Kevin said, "He may have offered to do that, and Christensen wouldn't go along with it."

I nodded. "That would be consistent with what I know about Dan. He wouldn't take a payoff."

Tim looked at Pete. "Do you think Goldstein was legit?"

"Yeah, I do. He was absolutely shocked and appalled to see Jamie's face. I don't believe he had prior knowledge of the trouble Jamie's been having. And Dan apparently didn't suspect him of being involved. But he could be a stellar actor, I guess."

"Hmm." Tim gave Pete a half-grin. "You were always one of the best at picking out the liars. But, yeah, theoretically he could still be on the suspect list." He wrote "Ben Goldstein-unlikely" under Andy's name.

The woman from HALT, Officer Passey, spoke up. "This doesn't sound like a situation that would fall under HALT's jurisdiction. We investigate fraudulent medical practice, and it doesn't sound like these guys are practicing medicine. They're just doing research, right?"

Tim said, "Right."

"Okay. However, it does sound like something the state medical board would be interested in. I'd definitely report it to them."

I raised my hand again. "We have to find out for certain who to report. I don't want to get Ben in trouble if he's not involved."

"Right." Passey smiled at me, stood up, and shouldered her bag. "Good luck. If you get in there and find out they've been doing experiments on people stashed in their back room, call me."

Everyone laughed uneasily.

"Okay." Tim set down his marker and rubbed his hands together. "Now we need to bring in all three of the doctors, separately, and have a talk with them. Goldstein first since he's the one we want to rule out. Everyone agreed on that?"

A consensus was reached, and the meeting broke up. I stood up and stretched gingerly. Kevin patted me on the shoulder and went back to work. Pete looked at me. "Anywhere else you want to go before we go home?"

"Could we stop by the library?"

"Yeah, but why?"

"I just want to put things there in order. I'll go back to work Monday. I want to have everything ready."

Pete grinned. "You're a little OCD, you know."

"Yeah, I know. Occupational hazard with librarians."

"Okay. If you're sure you're up to it."

"I am. Plus, this will let me tell everyone the story today, so I can actually work on Monday."

He laughed. "Oh, yeah. The telling of the tale will take a while. Dr. Loomis had better call a meeting."

It was close to noon, so we went to lunch first. When we got to the library, my face created quite a sensation. People gathered around and the word spread. In about five minutes, everyone that was able came to hear the story. That was fortunate; it meant I only had to tell it once. Everyone was astounded to hear that IT Andy had been involved, and that he wasn't cooperating with the police.

My office still looked funny without a PC on my desk. It did give me a chance to clear the entire surface, though. Pete helped me clean and straighten and get everything put away that I'd left out on Wednesday, thinking I'd be back on Thursday. I put the inhaler that I was carrying with me into my desk drawer to replace the one that I'd emptied on Monday. When we finished, my office was clean and organized, just like the day I'd moved into it. I stood back and admired our handiwork. "This is awesome. Thanks for helping."

Pete laughed. "You're welcome. It doesn't take much to make you happy, does it?"

I tried to grin; that still hurt. "I'm low maintenance. Give me milkshakes and a clean office and I'm all set."

Pete looked at the pictures I had on the top shelves of my bookcases. There was already one with him in it, from one of our hiking expeditions. He took it down and looked at it. "I remember this hike. That was the day we went too far and ended up in Encino."

"Yeah." I laughed. "I have to get some more pictures of you in here."

He put the picture back and looked at me gravely. "When Ben asked you yesterday if we were a couple, I wasn't sure what you were going to say."

"I know. I could feel you tense up when he asked." I reached out and took his hand. "I want to try this again with you. I want to be with you. I figure -" I stopped and took a breath. "I figure if you're the one that can hurt me, then you're the one I should be with. Because you're the one that -" I stopped again and looked right into his eyes. "Because you're the one."

Pete smiled. He did have a beautiful smile. "I'm glad you think so. Because I think you're the one, too." He laughed. "And it's making me crazy, not being able to kiss you with your mouth all swollen up like that."

I shook my head. "A couple of days. I'll be all better."

"Yeah, you will." He sighed and squeezed my hand. "Okay. Are we done here? You look exhausted. And I need to turn in grades by 6:00."

"Yeah, we're done." And I *was* exhausted. There was nothing I wanted more at that moment than a nap.

We got home a little after 2:30. I changed into sweats and got on the sofa with a book. Pete went up to the office to turn in his grades. I barely got through a paragraph before I was asleep.

When I woke up, it was 5:30 and Pete was gone.

I looked for a note. There wasn't one on the ottoman. I went up to the kitchen and looked on the dining table, the counter, and the fridge. No note. I went up to the office; there was nothing on the desk. There was no note lying on our bed, or written in soap on the bathroom mirror.

Nothing to indicate where he'd gone.

That was odd.

I went back downstairs and walked outside to where we parked our cars. The Jeep wasn't there.

Huh. Maybe he'd run to the grocery store and thought he'd be back before I woke up.

I went back inside and saw my phone lying on the ottoman. Maybe he'd sent me a text. I picked up the phone and unlocked the screen. I was right; there was a text message. But it wasn't from Pete.

It was from Ben Goldstein.

Found something big. Can't talk, have to see you. Meet me at lab asap.

But this text was sent to me, not Pete.

Pete must have seen the text when it came through and decided that he'd let me sleep and go meet Ben himself.

I called Pete's phone. It rang, then went to voicemail. I left a message - "Hey, where are you?" - then hung up. I texted him and waited a few minutes; no response.

Weird. If he was just at the lab talking to Ben, why wouldn't he answer?

Maybe they were in an elevator.

Or maybe something was wrong.

Shit. Had we been wrong about Ben?

There was one way to find out. I changed from sweats to jeans and a t-shirt, grabbed my wallet, phone and keys, and went out. It took me about 20 minutes in the Friday evening traffic to get to Cedars. I spotted Pete's Jeep in a parking space about halfway between the front door and the street. I pulled in next to it, cut the engine, and called Pete again. Same result. I texted him again; no response.

So I called Kevin. His phone went to voicemail, too. I left him a longer message, telling him where I was, what Ben's text had said, and that Pete's car was here and he wasn't answering his phone. Then I texted him - *911. Check your voicemail asap.*

I locked the car and went inside.

I took the stairs to the third floor. If anything bad was happening, I wanted to be able to come in through the back of the lab. I eased the door open and stuck my head through. The hallway was deserted. I could only see enough of the back door of the lab to see that there were lights on in there. The door to Dr. Oliver's office was to my immediate right; I tested the handle. Locked. I crossed the hall and put my ear to the door of the lab. I could hear voices, although I couldn't make out what they were saying.

There were two voices. One was male - low, calm. Pete's voice.

The other voice was raised and agitated.

And it was female.

Oh, shit.

I tried the handle of the door, very slowly and quietly. It didn't turn. I was going to have to go to the front door of the lab.

I sent Kevin another text. *I'm at lab. Can hear Pete and a woman. She sounds upset. I'm going in.* I turned my phone to silent mode and slid it into my pocket.

I went to the front door of the lab and tested the doorknob. It turned. I slowly, quietly eased the door open a crack and peeked in.

And found myself looking right down the barrel of a gun.

The door opened the rest of the way. Alana Wray backed up, keeping the pistol she was holding leveled at my face. "Finally. Get in here."

I went in.

"Turn around. Hands on your head."

I did what she said. She stuck the barrel of the gun right at the base of my skull, kicked the door closed and locked it.

What I saw sent a paralyzing jolt through me.

Ben Goldstein was slumped in the far corner of the lab, covered in blood from a head wound. Pete was in the center of the room, his wrists handcuffed behind him, locked around a supporting beam.

I looked at Pete. He narrowed his eyes and shook his head very slightly. *Don't do anything stupid.*

Wray gave me a little shove in the back. "Move. Down that aisle." She motioned me to the aisle one over from where Pete was chained to the post. "Turn around."

I turned and noted that Wray was wearing latex gloves. Wonderful. I took another look at the gun. A small .38. It occurred to me at that moment that we might not make it out of this. I prayed that Kevin was on his way.

Because Alana Wray was pissed. She was breathing fast and sweating and her face was flushed. She glared at me and yelled, practically spitting. "This is all *your fault*!"

"*My* fault?"

"Yes, *your* fault! You and Christensen! You...you...*fucking librarians!* You couldn't leave well enough alone, could you? Either one of you? Had to go snooping around in things that weren't your business. No one was getting hurt, no crimes were committed, but the two of you just couldn't let it *go!*"

I tried to look with my peripheral vision for anything I could use as a weapon. There was some glassware sitting on the countertops. Maybe I could palm something. "You've sure committed some crimes now. How did you kill Dan?"

"I injected him with potassium. Right through one of the holes left over from those ridiculous piercings. That should have ended it." She was pacing a little bit now, but not lowering the gun. I still didn't think I could make a move to do anything without getting shot. "How did you find out about it, anyway?"

I couldn't think of a reason not to tell her. "He mailed me a letter with the two citations and asked me to look into it."

She stopped pacing for a second and pointed the gun back directly at me. "I was monitoring all the mail going out of his office. How did he get it to you?"

"The postmark was Malibu."

She snorted. "Mailed from Ben's house. Should have known." She started pacing again, muttering to herself.

I needed to keep her talking, to try to keep her off balance if I could. But I didn't want to make her so mad that she'd just shoot me. "Who is Andy Mitchell to you?"

She stopped, surprised, then sneered. "Well, aren't you the smart one. Andy is my nephew. My older sister's son. For a little extra cash he was more than happy to monitor your computer for me."

"UCLA knows about that. He's going to lose his job."

She waved the gun, almost airily. "Not my problem."

So much for family ties. "What did Ben find out?"

"He found out that I'd been married before. And that my previous married name was Collinsworth. And that there had been an Alana Collinsworth doing a post-doctoral fellowship in fertility medicine in Oxford in 2002."

Damn. It hadn't occurred to me to investigate her background that closely. "How'd he find that out?"

"Tristan told him, the old fool."

"Where is Dr. Oliver? Do you have him tied up somewhere too?"

She laughed. "Of course not. I need him. He's gone to Seattle for the weekend."

"Does he know about the plagiarism?"

"Don't be ridiculous. That old fart wouldn't know a stem cell if it showed up in his oatmeal. I don't think he even read the article we supposedly co-wrote. He's here for fundraising purposes, nothing else."

Wray was calming down and relaxing her guard a bit. I spotted a long test tube lying on the counter near the edge. If I could get her to look away from me, I could snatch it quickly. "Is Ben dead?"

She looked over at him; I swiftly palmed the test tube and tried to curl my fingers around it without being obvious. "No, he's still breathing. For now."

She was going to kill us, no doubt. I had to stall her. Kevin would come. "So what's your plan here?"

That got her mad again. "I had a plan, and your boyfriend here wrecked it! So now I have to get rid of all three of you!" She stopped and took a deep breath. "The plan was that Ben would text you, you would come here and identify him as the plagiarist, you and he would struggle, the gun would go off and kill Ben, and you'd be overcome by his cologne and die. He -" she waved the gun at Pete, "wasn't supposed to be involved at all. Now I have to come up with something else."

Pete hadn't spoken to this point; now he did. "Why not just shoot us all and flee the country?"

What the *fuck* was he thinking? I stared at him. He looked back at me and shook his head slightly again.

Wray focused on him. I used the opportunity to move a couple of feet closer to a rack full of test tubes on the counter to my right. "Because I have to keep the lab open. I can't let any of this interfere with my research."

Pete was using his calm, reasonable psychologist voice. "Aren't there easier ways to make money?"

Wray shouted so loudly it startled me and I almost dropped the large test tube. "*It's not about the money!*" If there was anyone in this end of the building, they'd hear her. Hell, they might have heard her in the parking lot.

Pete didn't raise his voice. "So what is it about?"

Wray advanced on Pete a bit. I took the chance of gently sliding the rack of test tubes closer to the edge of the counter. "It's about the *research!* The procedure will work! We're close! We just have to keep working at it, which means the lab has to stay open, which means I can't be implicated in any of this!"

Pete was taking over the conversation so I could move around more. "But..."

"*Shut up!* You have no idea what this is about!"

"What is it about? Tell me."

"Trying to keep me talking, eh?" She laughed bitterly. "Okay, fine. You have no idea what it's like to be a woman who wants a child of her *own.* A child with her own genes." Her voice caught. "This research is the *chance* for all those women. If I can create ova from stem cells, those women can have children. Their *own* children, rather than children created from some other woman's eggs."

Whoa. I wondered if she was including herself in that group. Pete asked, "So why plagiarize Hughes and Llewellyn's work? I don't understand why you couldn't have just built on their work rather than stealing it outright."

"Because I didn't have *time!*" Yelling again. "The grant money was only going to fund us for two years. We needed results by that time or the funding would disappear. We were nowhere near producing results on our own. So I had to fake them, and it was easier to do it with Hughes's article. It was in Welsh. No one would ever have known." She waved the gun around some more. "Those fucking *bastards* wouldn't add me as an author on their pathetic article. I worked in that lab right along with them, and they gave me no credit for it whatsoever. They didn't want to tarnish my name with failure, they said. Bullshit! They had no imagination at all. I offered Llewellyn a job, at this lab, and he wouldn't take it. I gave him two chances, and he said no to both of them. So it was *his fault*."

Accepting blame was not this woman's strong suit. I suddenly realized something. "You killed Llewellyn, didn't you?"

"The car accident killed him. I just ran him off the road. Hughes had the good graces to have a heart attack on his own before I published my article. Saved me the trouble of going back to Oxford to deal with him." She glared at me. "You're one of them, aren't you? Uptight Oxford misogynist bastards?"

"I went to Oxford. None of that other stuff." Her focus was back on me now. I moved to the other side of the aisle, away from Pete, and she circled around the end of the lab bench after me.

"Thought so. I think I'll just kill you now." She reached into the pocket of her lab coat.

Shit. I thought of one more tactic. "You learned a lot about me from my work computer, but you didn't learn everything. Do you know that my brother is an LAPD homicide detective?"

Her head jerked up, and she stared at me, then laughed. "I don't believe you."

"Oh, it's true. You're not so damn smart, as it turns out. My big brother is Detective Kevin Brodie, West LA division. And my boyfriend is his former partner. So you're about to murder an ex-cop and the brother of a cop. LAPD is going to be on you like fleas on a dog. You won't get away with killing us, so why do it?"

"Oh, I think I'll get away with it." She pulled her hand out of her pocket and showed me a bottle of Drakkar Noir cologne.

I blanched, and she saw it. "The doctor that treated you in the emergency room was very thorough. This is exactly the same cologne that caused your attack last week." She seemed more relaxed now, and I didn't think that was a good thing. "I've worked out what's going to happen here. A ménage a trois. So sad. Ben, as it turns out, was our plagiarist. Dan found out about it and was investigating, so Ben killed him. But Dan had told you, and you uncovered the articles. Although you suspected Tristan, Ben was nervous. He decided he needed to get rid of you as well, so he lured you here. But Ferguson intercepted the text and thought you were meeting Ben for a tryst. He came to confront Ben, but Ben had a gun, forced boyfriend to handcuff himself to the post, then shot him. You arrived, found your boyfriend dead, went crazy, attacked Ben, and were overcome by his cologne." She walked over to Ben and sprayed a considerable amount of the cologne on his upper body. The scent started wafting toward me, and I felt my airways start to react. "Ben, poor soul, faced with the carnage, knew he'd never get away with it, so he shot himself in the head." She turned back to me and advanced, spraying as she came.

I heard sounds out in the hallway. Someone was yelling, and there were feet running. Pete started yelling for help. I picked up the rack of test tubes and threw it at her. She ducked, but got nicked by some broken glass. She charged me, spraying from the cologne bottle as she came. I buried my nose in my bent elbow and turned to run. I didn't realize that there was a step stool in my path, and I tripped over it. I righted myself, but that gave her just enough time to catch up to me. She yanked my arm away from my face and hit me full force with the spray, emptying the bottle. She dropped it and ran for the back door of the lab.

I couldn't hold my breath any longer, and I had to breathe in some of the perfume. She'd soaked my shirt with it thoroughly. I felt my airways start to react and started to wheeze. And in my haste, I'd forgotten to bring an inhaler with me. With the condition I was already in, it didn't take long for me to tip over into a full blown attack. I bent over at the waist, but it didn't help. I was losing ground fast. I dragged myself to the aisle and got on my hands and knees, then started crawling to the front door of the lab. There was pounding on the door and more shouting. I collapsed face down on the ground. I heard a crash, a gunshot, and a scream. And then I was gone.

Chapter 12
Saturday, June 9

It was dark.

I was alone.

It wasn't completely dark.

There was light leaking around the curtains in front of me.

There were curtains.

I was in a room.

A very small room.

I was sitting up, partially.

There was a rhythmic hissing sound coming from just behind me.

My eyes began to adjust.

I tried to look to my right, but I couldn't move my head very far.

There was something pinching my finger.

I tried to raise my hand to look at it, and I couldn't.

There was something in my mouth.

I tried to swallow and couldn't.

I tried to breathe, and heard the hissing sound again.

Huh.

I went back to sleep.

The next time I opened my eyes, there was more light. There was also someone in my room.

A young woman in mint green scrubs was to my right, making notations on a clipboard. She looked down at me, and smiled. "Well, hi there."

I tried to say something but couldn't. There was something in my mouth. And there was that hissing sound again.

"Don't try to talk. You've got a tube down your throat." The young woman leaned on the rail on my bed. "My name's Melissa. I'm your nurse today. You're in the intensive care unit at UCLA hospital. You've been here since last night." She patted my arm. "I want you to blink once for yes, twice for no. Can you do that?"

I blinked once.

"Great. Do you remember what happened to you?"

Did I? Oh, yeah. Alana Wray in the lab with a bottle of cologne. I blinked once.

"Excellent." She smiled down at me. "You're doing great. You're breathing on your own, and your oxygen levels are getting better. The ventilator is just helping you out to rest your breathing muscles. Are you having any discomfort anywhere?"

Actually, no. I blinked twice.

"Great." She patted me again. "Your family is all out in the waiting room. Would you like to see one of them?"

I blinked once.

"Okay. I'll go get them." She pushed aside the curtain at the foot of my bed and left. It turned out there wasn't a wall there, just a curtain. I could see a piece of counter with someone sitting behind it at a computer, and a clock. 10:30. Was that AM or PM? No way to tell in here. But she said I'd been here since last night - maybe it was AM now.

Melissa reappeared with Pete in tow, his arm in a sling.

Oh wow. I'd felt curiously calm until now, but the sight of Pete ended that. I tried to reach out to him and realized my hands were tied down.

Melissa untied me quickly. "Sorry about that. We didn't want you to wake up confused and try to pull your tube out." She patted Pete on his good shoulder. Lots of patting going on. "I can give you ten minutes. Oh, and he blinks once for yes, twice for no." She left, pulling the curtain closed again.

I reached out again. Pete took the hand without the IV in and held it against his chest while he kissed me on the forehead. He looked awful - rumpled, scruffy, red-eyed. I'd never seen a more beautiful sight.

His voice was rough. "You scared the *shit* out of me."

I blinked once.

"How do you feel? Oh, that's not yes or no. Are you feeling bad?"

Not too bad, considering. I blinked twice.

He let go of the hand that had the oxygen meter on it and brushed my hair off my forehead. "You're doing fine, they say. Your doctor will be in later, and they'll probably take you off the machine."

I blinked once.

"You probably want to know what happened, huh?"

I sure did. I blinked once, and nodded as much as I could.

"Kevin and Tim broke through the door as you were going down. Kevin tackled Wray as she turned to shoot me and knocked off her aim."

Oh my God. Pete had almost died. I couldn't make a sound, but I thrashed around a little bit. He got my meaning and shook his head. "It's okay. It went through my deltoid muscle, near the skin, didn't even hit any bone."

It most definitely *wasn't* okay, but we'd have to discuss it later. I blinked once.

"They've arrested Wray for the murder of Dan and the attempted murder of you, me, and Ben."

Ben was okay? I needed to communicate. I made a writing motion.

"Uh - okay, hang on." Pete stuck his head out of the curtain and asked for a pen and paper. He came back with it and handed it to me. I was at a weird angle to write, but I managed to spell out "Ben's okay?"

"Yeah. He's got a concussion and lost a good bit of blood, but he'll be fine."

I wrote, "Wray confessed?"

"No. She's lawyered up, and Andy still isn't talking. But since we're all alive and well, she has no chance of getting away with anything."

I blinked once and laid down the paper. The burst of adrenaline that had shot through me when I saw Pete was already failing me. Pete started to say something else, but Melissa came back in. “Sorry, guys, but I’ve got to limit you to ten minutes per hour.”

“Okay.” Pete kissed my forehead. “I’ll see you later. Don’t go anywhere.”

I’d have stuck my tongue out at him if I could.

I must have dozed back off, because the next thing I knew, my dad was in the room. “Hey, you.” He reached over and squeezed my hand. “How are you feeling?”

I made a see-saw motion with my hand and pantomimed pulling the breathing tube out.

My dad nodded. “Yeah - your doctor stuck his head in a little while ago and said he’d be back. I think he’s planning to do that.”

I picked up the paper and pen from where they’d fallen on my lap. “What time is it?”

“It’s 1:30. You went back to sleep for a while.”

Jeez. I did more than doze off, then. I wrote, “Any confessions?”

“Nope, not yet. Although Kevin figures they can get the young guy to agree to a deal. His parents are leaning on him pretty hard to do that.”

The curtain parted, and Dr. Weikal strode in. “There he is, wide awake! How are you feeling?”

I made the same see-saw motion and pointed at the tube.

“Yes. First I need to take a look at your oxygenation...” He pressed a button on one of the machines to my right, and a strip of paper printed out. He looked it over. “Very good. You’ve been at more than 90% saturation for several hours now.” He moved to my side. “Okay, here’s what I’m going to do. I’m going to unhook the ventilator, and listen to your lungs while you’ve still got the tube in. If it sounds good, we’ll take it out.” He unfastened the tube and moved it to the side.

I took in a breath on my own. My rib muscles were sore. It felt a bit strange to not have the machine kick in. I'd grown that accustomed to it in such a short time.

"Okay, sit forward a little for me." I did. Dr. Weikal put his stethoscope in his ears and placed the flat piece on my back. "Take a deep breath, in and out."

I breathed several times. He moved the stethoscope around, listening closely, then stepped back and pulled the earpieces out. "Sounds good. Does it feel all right?"

I nodded.

"Okay, then, let's get that thing out." He slowly and gently pulled all the tape loose from my face, deflated the little balloon that was hanging from the tube, and got a firm grip on the tube itself. "Now, take in another breath - now breathe out." As I breathed out, he pulled.

Ugh. It felt as bad as I had imagined, but it was over quickly. I had a coughing fit, and Dr. Weikal poured me a glass of water. "Okay?"

I drank, handed the glass back, and managed to croak out, "Okay." It hurt to talk.

"Your throat and voice are going to be a little scratchy for a while, but that should clear up pretty quickly. We'll keep you on liquids for today - milkshakes, soup, ice cream. If everything goes well for the rest of the day, you can go to a regular room in the morning."

"Not home?"

"Not tomorrow. You were in severe status asthmaticus. If everything still looks good tomorrow, you can go home Monday. Stay hydrated. Respiratory therapy will be around with a nebulizer treatment soon."

I leaned back against the pillows. "Awesome."

He grinned. "Great. The nurse will come in a few minutes to take this away -" he patted the ventilator - "and hook up a tube to give you some oxygen flow through your nose. I'll come back and check on you this evening."

Nurse Melissa came to collect the ventilator and my dad. I spent the next several hours getting nebulizers, drinking water, and eating ice cream. I hadn't thought about peeing until I'd been awake a few hours, at which point Pete helpfully pointed out that I had a catheter in. Great – another tube that would have to be pulled out.

That happened the next morning – yeowch! – and I was transferred to a regular room. I was still getting nebulizers but didn't have to use the oxygen anymore. My oxygenation had dropped back into the 80s after the ventilator tube came out, but never got lower than that. And I did get to go home on Monday morning.

I went to Pete's long enough to pack, then went home with my dad to Oceanside. I spent the next week there, breathing in the clean sea air and helping my dad in the garden. Pete came down on Wednesday after SMC's graduation. The following Monday, June 18, we went back to Santa Monica.

Almost four weeks after the fire, Kevin and Abby moved back in to our apartment. I kept paying my third of the rent so they could afford to stay in our apartment until the lease was up. It worked out okay since Pete didn't have a mortgage for me to help out with.

Alana Wray maintained her innocence for about a week. Then, under pressure from his parents, Andy Mitchell gave in and told the police that Alana had hired him to sabotage my computer and trash my office. It turned out that Alana's older sister, Andy's mother, had been estranged from Alana for years, and Andy's dad hated Alana's guts. They weren't about to let their son take the rap for his aunt.

Better than that, Andy knew the identity of "Ed," who had beaten me up and, as it turned out, had been following me from the time I requested the Welsh article. He'd also been the one who had slashed my tires at Cedars. "Ed" was a cousin of Alana's, Wayne

Edward Sobrowski. The police found him easily enough. He refused to talk until he found out that Alana was going to blame *him* for everything. Then he spilled the whole story.

Andy didn't get jail time, but he did get two years' probation and lost his job. Sobrowski pled guilty to conspiracy to commit aggravated arson and was sentenced to twelve years. Mauro Politano, who'd broken in to the apartment and condo, was sentenced to eight years in prison for the two first degree burglaries and another eight years for felony arson.

Once Alana learned that both Andy and Wayne had admitted everything and were prepared to testify against her, she pled guilty to the first degree murder of Dan Christensen and the attempted murders of Ben, Pete, and me. She was sentenced to life without parole and shipped off to Chowchilla.

Diane DeLong did lose her job in the public schools. Liz heard through the grapevine that she'd gotten hired at a private high school in Riverside and had moved to the Inland Empire. Liz also heard that Diane had dyed her Mohawk bright blue.

Life settled back down into a routine of sorts, even though it was a new routine. Most mornings, Pete and I went for a run, down to the beach and to the pier and back, sometimes farther. Instead of walking to work, I rode the bus. We still spent most of our Saturdays hiking. Pete cooked, I cleaned. Life was good.

I went back to work on a Thursday. I was sorting through two weeks of accumulated mail – again! – when Ben Goldstein showed up at my office. He'd sent me a get-well card, but I hadn't seen him since.

I stood up to greet him. "Hey, how are you? Come in." We shook hands and I offered him a seat.

"I'm fine, thanks." He looked around my office at the walls lined with books and photos. "This is nice."

"Thanks, I like it. What brings you here?"

"I wanted to touch base. See how you were doing and what had happened with the case."

I filled him in on the outcome. "And I'm fine, thanks." I smiled at him. "How are you doing?"

"Oh, okay, I guess. Now that it's all over, it's finally settling in on me that Dan's gone." He looked at his feet. "I really miss him."

"I'm sure. I can't imagine."

Ben looked up at me, sideways. "He told me that you and he were involved."

"Very briefly. Years ago. When I got his letter, it had been three years since I'd seen him."

He nodded. "He said he was a different person before he met me."

"I - um - I was in his office after he died and saw the picture of the two of you. Looked like you were on an island, somewhere? He looked different in that picture from when I'd known him."

Ben smiled sadly. "That was a great trip. That was where we really came together as a couple." He sighed and looked out my office door into the distance. "I still can't believe what happened."

"Me either."

He looked back at me. "I'm leaving town."

"You are? I guess that's a good idea?"

"It is. The lab is finished, obviously, Dr. Oliver is retiring, and I've lost my taste for research. Word has gotten around here about what happened, and even though there's no speculation that I was involved at all, everyone knows I'm innocent, I just think it would be better for me to make a clean start somewhere else."

"Where are you going?"

"Baltimore. I'm going to practice OB-GYN. Deliver babies and all that." He smiled, a little self-consciously.

"That's great." I smiled back. "LA's loss will be Baltimore's gain. I hear it's nice there."

"Yeah. It's on the water, near DC, not far from New York where I have family. Lots of advantages."

"Well, that's great." I wasn't sure what else to say.

He looked down and rubbed the carpet with his toe. "I also wanted to thank you for carrying out Dan's request. I don't think I said that before. I know he didn't involve me from the start because he was trying to protect me. And if there wasn't anything to his suspicions, then he wouldn't have had to ever say anything to me about it."

"So he didn't know about the plagiarism already?"

"No. He suspected it, but he hadn't been able to get the Welsh article in its entirety, so he didn't know for sure. He did know that the calculations in our article didn't add up; he'd gotten that far." He grimaced. "I went to see Alana before her sentencing. She knew Dan was sniffing around, because she knew that he'd tried to access the Welsh article, and she didn't want to let him get far enough to alert me. And she wasn't sure that he hadn't."

"So he left you the information that he'd gathered to that point."

"Yes. And he wrote you the letter, because he was paranoid, but also because he was determined to get to the bottom of it. And he trusted you to do that."

I was taken aback. "Really?"

"Yes." Ben smiled, sadly. "He did. I know you and he didn't end well, but he was impressed with your professionalism. Your librarianship, he called it. He said that you were working on his 'problem,' as he called it, and I should talk to you. That I should trust you."

"Wow." Once again, Dan had surprised me. "I had no idea that he thought of me in any positive terms whatsoever."

Ben's smiled widened a bit. "I'm sure you didn't. Dan kept his feelings close to the vest. But that's what he told me. And there's one thing that Dan was *not*, and that was a liar."

"That's very true."

Ben stood. “I don’t want to keep you. I’m leaving town tomorrow, and I didn’t want to leave without saying goodbye, and thank you.”

I stood too. “Thank *you.* And good luck. If there’s ever anything I can do for you, let me know.”

Ben nodded. “I will. And tell Pete goodbye for me as well.”

I said I would, and Ben left. I glanced at the clock. 12:45 – almost time for my reference shift. I hit the coffee shop for a mochaccino, then met Liz at the desk.

It wasn’t busy, now that summer had started. I was working on some research for a faculty member when Clinton appeared.

“Hi, Clinton.”

“The word for the day is *exultation.*” He bowed, and straightened back up.

Then he winked at me.

Acknowledgements

I couldn't have done this without my fellow members of the Faculty Fiction Writing Group: Becca, Michelle, the two Michael F.'s, and Trey, who all read the first three chapters and gave me great feedback. Thanks, guys! Enormous thanks, as well, to Dustin and Cheryl, who read the entire book and also gave me invaluable feedback. This is a much better book, thanks to them. And extra, special, awesome thanks to Chris, who must have read this four times, and found something to fix every time.

Turn the page for a preview of *Hoarded to Death*, Jamie Brodie Mystery #2.

Hoarded to Death

September 2012

"Today, on *Clean My Hoard...*"

An obese young woman, sitting in a chair on a rickety front porch. "My name is Tami, and I'm a hoarder."

Tami continued to speak as a camera panned around a room piled to the ceiling with boxes, bags, clothes, and garbage. "If I don't clean up my house, I'm gonna lose my kids."

A little girl, about six years old. "I hate the way my house looks. I wish mommy would clean up."

The camera switched to Tami and another woman yelling at each other. Tami: "I won't let you take away my kids!" The other woman: "You won't have any choice if you don't clean up this mess!"

The title screen appeared, then a commercial started. I hit the fast forward button on the remote.

It was Sunday morning. We'd spent all day yesterday on a friend's boat fishing and drinking beer. Today I was mildly sunburned and hung over. Pete was tanned and less hung over. We'd planned to go hiking today, but it had turned cold and foggy and we'd decided to stay in.

I was on the sofa; Pete was on the floor in front of me. I was massaging his left shoulder. Back in June, Pete was shot in an attempt on my life. He'd finished physical therapy but still had some muscle stiffness. Especially after a day of fishing.

I'd moved in with former boyfriend Pete Ferguson on an emergency basis three and a half months ago after my apartment was vandalized and set on fire. We'd dated for a while several years ago, and had remained friends. I'd gone through a couple of other boyfriends since then, and I was glad to be back with Pete. We'd settled into a cozy domesticity.

But it still felt temporary to me. I was continuing to pay rent on my old apartment, since my other roommates, my brother Kevin and his girlfriend Abby, couldn't swing the entire rent payment on their own. The time was coming in a few weeks when we'd have to either renew the lease on our two-bedroom apartment, or Kevin and Abby would have to sign a new lease on a one-bedroom. I was facing a major decision.

Pete said he loved me. And I cared a lot about him. We got along great. There was absolutely no reason that I should be worried about the future.

So why was I?

The commercials were over, and I hit the play button. Tami the hoarder was talking as the camera panned around her house in more detail. What a mess.

I just didn't understand the desire to gather stuff. When our apartment had been set on fire, it was my belongings that were torched. I'd lost everything except my computer, my car, and the clothes on my back. Starting with a clean slate was refreshing, in a way. I didn't have nearly as much stuff now, and I was perfectly happy. It gave me a sense of freedom. It was a lot easier to decide what to wear to work when you had fewer choices. And I hadn't worn a tie in two and a half months.

I picked up the remote to fast forward through the commercials again. "Okay, take your pick. Does she lose her kids or not? By the end of the show?"

Pete mulled it over. "I say no."

"All right. Then I say yes."

Clean My Hoard was a show that we never failed to watch. We both found it fascinating, but for different reasons. Pete was a psychologist, an assistant professor at Santa Monica College, and it was instructive for him to watch personality disorders in action. For me, my brother Kevin's ex-wife, Jennifer, was a hoarder. It was one of the reasons they divorced. Since then I'd always been morbidly fascinated by the hoarding shows. It was like watching a train wreck.

It was sick humor on our part, but Pete and I would always bet on the outcome of the show. Would the lady lose her kids? Would the man lose his house? Would the husband divorce his wife? The loser of the bet had to clean the baseboards of the townhouse that week.

Pete and I were both neat by nature. We didn't have many characteristics of stereotypical gay guys, but that was one of them. We liked a clean house - although Pete's passion for cleanliness didn't match mine - and we didn't mind cleaning. But we both hated doing baseboards. So that's what we bet for.

By the end of the show, Tami hadn't yet lost her kids. She'd cleaned up enough of the house to satisfy her sister, who was the one threatening to call Child Protective Services.

I'd be cleaning baseboards this week.

Monday morning, after going for a run and cleaning the baseboards, I hurried to the bus stop. I was a librarian at UCLA's Young Research Library, with a subject specialty in ancient history. The fall quarter was starting in a week, and I had a lot to do. I spent the morning at my desk, updating our online research guides, filling information requests from faculty who'd been off all summer, and working on a proposal for an upcoming conference. At 1:00, I went to the reference desk for my regular two-hour shift. My partner on the desk and best friend at work, Liz Nguyen, met me there.

At precisely 1:30, our regular eccentric Clinton approached the desk.

Liz said, "Hi, Clinton."

He regarded us gravely and said, "The word of the day is *rectitude*." He bowed at the waist and strode away.

Clinton performed this service daily, Monday through Friday, rain or shine. Liz and I had improved our respective vocabularies greatly as a result.

Liz looked up *rectitude*. She laughed. "It says, 'The quality or state of being straight.'"

"No *way*." I snickered. "Well, he was half right."

"It also means righteousness."

"Ah. So you're straight and I'm righteous."

We both got tickled and had to pull ourselves back together for the next patron.

When I got back to my office shortly after 3:00, there was a message on my phone. "Hello, Mr. Brodie, this is Raven Hechesky. I'm the assistant producer for the TV show *Clean My Hoard*."

What??

"We have an application for our show from Jennifer Graham, and she has listed you as one of the people she'd like to have on her support team as she goes through this process. I'd like to meet with you this week, at your convenience." She left her number.

Holy *shit*. My brother's ex was going to clean up her mess? On national TV? And she wanted *me* to help her? And she'd taken back her maiden name. Was that a sign that Jennifer was getting her act together?

My brother Kevin had met Jennifer Graham in college, here at UCLA. Jennifer had grown up on the edge of poverty in a double-wide mobile home in Julian, California, a tiny town of a few hundred people in the mountains of San Diego County. I hadn't gotten to know her well. While she and Kevin were dating, I was in college at Berkeley. A year after they got married, I moved to Oxford, England, to begin graduate school.

I could count the number of times I'd interacted with Jennifer on both hands, including the wedding. She'd always seemed a bit standoffish. Or maybe she was just shy. Either way, we didn't talk much – but for some reason I'd always felt sorry for her. Even after the divorce.

My dad started mentioning problems in Kevin and Jennifer's relationship during my third year at Oxford, but I was having problems in my own relationship with my longtime boyfriend and couldn’t worry too much about what was going on with Kevin. My boyfriend broke up with me, I graduated from Oxford, and moved to LA for library school. Kevin and Jennifer finalized their divorce, and Kevin and I moved in together. I hadn’t heard anything of Jennifer since. She and Kevin hadn’t had kids, so there was no reason for them to stay in contact.

Before I agreed to see Raven Hechesky, I had to get the okay from Kevin. If he didn’t want me to participate, there was no point in meeting with Raven.

Might as well find out now.

CPSIA information can be obtained
at www.ICGtesting.com
Printed in the USA
BVOW06s1921131117
500313BV00009B/452/P

9 781522 760009